The Immortality Clause

Abigail Hawk

CLAUDIA BELL #1 OF THE IMMORTELLE SERIES

Second Edition (v2.00)

Dedication

Dedicated to Adrienne & Darian Smith, for your support, encouragement, and grammatical nitpicking.
I love you guys!

Abigail Hawk

THE IMMORTELLE
The Immortality Clause
At First Blush

V. L. Dreyer

THE SURVIVORS
The Survivors Book I: Summer
The Survivors Book II: Autumn
The Survivors Book III: Winter
The Survivors Book IV: Spring

Chapter One

Claudia Bell stared at her reflection in the mirror, and decided that whoever thought elevators should have mirrored walls must have been a genius. The trip up felt like it was taking forever, but at least the mirror gave her something to do besides try to smother her nerves. At least when she was busy touching up her makeup, she wasn't wasting time on pointless worrying.

She was an attractive young woman, and she knew it, because she spent hours perfecting what nature had given her. Practicing law was still a man's game and her looks gave her power, because they were a means to make people instinctively underestimate her. Her looks were a weapon in her arsenal, nothing more. The hours that she spent with hair straighteners or at the nail salon were no different to a knight who spent his evenings sharpening his sword.

When her opponents looked at her, all they saw was a pretty young thing with immaculately-coiffed blonde hair and flawless makeup, dressed to the nines in the latest business fashions. Most of them dismissed her without a second thought. What they didn't see was the razor wit that lay behind her deliberately-machinated insipid smile. People tended to relax when they saw her and assume she was nothing more than a blonde bimbo that somehow managed to muddle, or sleep her way through a law degree. Even other

1

women. No, *especially* other women.

While her foes were busy curling their lip and rolling their eyes, Claudia was watching them, assessing them, divining their weaknesses from the tiniest hints of body language and establishing the best strategy to use those weaknesses against them. Her enemies rarely realised just how intelligent she was until she dove for the metaphorical kill - and by then it was too late.

That was what made her so good at her job.

After what felt like an eon, the elevator reached its destination, and the doors popped open with a soft, pleasant chime. Claudia straightened her shoulders, adjusted her purse over her shoulder and settled her favourite vague, girlish smile onto her lips. This time there was no need. The man that greeted her had already seen what lay beneath her disguise, and felt the cut of her intellect. He'd fallen for her wiles in her first interview, and come out the other side feeling like less of a man. Which was exactly why he'd hired her.

"Ms Bell," he greeted her amiably, and offered her a hand to shake. She took it without hesitation, silently pleased by the gesture. Few people offered her the simple courtesy of a handshake until they considered her an equal. Most people greeted her as an inferior without even realising that they were doing it, treating her with broad gestures, bland smiles, and a hand on the small of the back.

"Mr Logan," she replied. "I'm flattered that you came to meet me personally."

"After that interview, how could I not?" he said. William Logan was a tall, older gentleman with grey hair and a neatly-trimmed beard. His lips curled into an amused smile, then he swiftly changed the subject and gestured towards the younger man at his side. "May I introduce you to Lucio Cavenelli? You'll be serving as his aide while you learn the ropes around here."

"Please, call me Luke," he said, offering his hand to her. "It's a pleasure to meet you."

She was well-versed in the art of reading body language, and she could see, written in his poise, that he was both curious about her and respectful of her. That also amused her, because it meant this man had been warned in advance not to underestimate her.

Now, that was a feeling she *really* liked.

"Likewise. I look forward to working with you." She shook his hand and used the moment to study the young man with an impartial eye. He was a little older than she was, perhaps a few years past thirty, but his appearance was youthful. His hair was jet black, slicked back from a face that was handsome and angular. Much like herself, he was dressed impeccably in a well-tailored business suit, his face was clean-shaven, and his hands were well-groomed.

The thing that interested her most was his eyes, though. In stark contrast to his dark hair and olive skin, his eyes were a particularly vivid shade of blue. In spite of herself, she found herself momentarily fascinated by them, until he spoke again and disrupted her thoughts.

"After what William's told me about your interview, I'm a little frightened to be working with you," he said, his words laced with pleasant humour to break the ice, a social grace that she appreciated.

"Oh, no need for that," she said with a chuckle and a playfully-wicked smile. "I only use my powers for good, never for evil."

The men both laughed at her joke, since they knew full well that was not the case. They were lawyers, after all. Manipulating people was what they excelled at. To be where she was — a graduate that held multiple degrees, and had interned at one of the most powerful law firms in Australasia for several years — she had to be just as wicked as they were.

"Luke, why don't you give Ms Bell the tour, and then show her to her office?" William Logan said, glancing at the younger man.

Another illusion: the illusion of choice. They may be friendly and bantering now, but Mr Logan was the head of the Legal Department and it was his whims to which they both danced. Luke was diplomatic enough not to point that out, of course. He just nodded and smiled, and beckoned for Claudia to follow him. She said a brief, polite farewell to her new employer and then followed the young man away from the elevator.

"I'm sure I don't need to tell you that this is the lobby," Luke said, gesturing around them. "If you need anything done, feel free to ask one of the receptionists. They're here to help."

"Of course." Claudia glanced at the trio of unsmiling women behind the reception desk and gave them a nod of greeting. Two of them were busy speaking into their wireless headsets and didn't seem to notice her at all, but the third looked up and returned the nod. Above them, the company logo was emblazoned on the marble wall: Cornelius Pharmaceuticals.

What a pretentious name, she thought snidely, and not for the first time. However, the pay was excellent, and part of her contract with her mother required her to spend some time working overseas, before she could earn her partnership in the family firm.

Her mother had found out about the opening at Cornelius through her connections in the industry, and she'd made all the arrangements for the interview. The company was located in the central business district of Auckland, New Zealand, just three hours from Brisbane by plane. At first, Claudia had been dubious about leaving her home and moving to such a small, isolated country, but she had always longed to travel and see the world. New Zealand was exotic enough to interest her, but similar enough to home to feel familiar. She'd flown over for the interview and found herself intrigued by the vast, open green spaces and the quirky people. When William Logan called to offer her the job, she'd accepted without hesitation.

Luke led her onwards, past the luxuriant leather couches and expensive art that hung around the waiting area, familiar to her after her interview two weeks before. Her stiletto heels clicked ominously on the hard tiles, and she relished the sound. The shoes might be impractical but they made her feel powerful, and she loved the way that people watched her when she wore them.

Like right now, in fact. Luke held open the door for her and she could feel his eyes on her as she passed through it, admiring her curves. Her jacket was carefully tailored to fit her physique, and the skirt was cut just short enough to show a generous portion of her long, shapely legs without being risqué.

At just the right moment, she shot a look back over her shoulder to catch him in the act. His head jerked up in surprise and his gaze snapped to her face. She raised a brow pointedly. He glanced away, with a faint smile dancing across his lips.

To her surprise, the moment left her vaguely uncomfortable, though she usually enjoyed catching people out when they least expected it. This time, it felt different. His smile said he knew something that she didn't. That was a feeling she did not care for at all.

***

Luke Cavenelli suddenly found himself fighting down the urge to laugh. She'd caught him with such an obvious ploy in spite of all his experience with women, and the advance warning from his elder. At nearly a century of age, he really should have known better.

And yet, she has no idea, he thought to himself as his gaze flicked away, amusement playing across his lips despite his best efforts to restrain it. *No idea who or what I am, no idea why she's really here.*

He felt a little guilty taking advantage of her ignorance, since he'd found the young lawyer to be interesting so far. She was so vivacious and full of life. He didn't much care for the plan that his elders had concocted, but at least she was entertaining to deal with. Despite his age, he was one of the youngest of his clan. Eternity and arrogance had not robbed him of his humanity just yet.

But, whether he liked her or not, there was politics to be considered. There was always politics.

"Through there is the cafeteria," he said absently, gesturing down one of the corridors. "But, the legal team generally go out for lunch. There's a diverse selection of restaurants and cafes in this area."

"So I noticed," she said. The young woman's voice was a crisp hybrid of British and Australian accents, which he knew was courtesy of the tutors her mother had insisted on hiring for her. Luke watched her while she wasn't looking, admiring the way her clothing was cut to accentuate her sensual curves rather than hide them. Long legs flowed into wickedly sharp heels, yet despite that she moved with a grace that was almost predatory. Her hair shone, coifed into shoulder length white-blonde curls in a style that reminded him poignantly of Maria.

Maria. The woman who had almost become his wife. He rarely thought of her these days; the Cabal seemed to consume his every waking thought. Again, he pushed the thoughts of his lost love back into the recesses of his memory, as he had done every time for the last seventy-five years. She was no longer a part of his reality.

This woman, though. This woman he found interesting, even fascinating. She was so unlike the immortal women that generally surrounded him. As the years rolled by, they tended to grow either depressed or arrogant. The depressed ones usually retreated within themselves, until finally the longing for death became overwhelming. The arrogant ones, on the other hand, regarded him as an undisciplined young stallion. They had no use for him unless they wanted to take him for a ride. Although most men in his position would have been perfectly happy with that arrangement, Luke was an old-fashioned kind of guy and hated being used for his body. He'd grown up in an era where you married young, and you stayed married. Divorce was simply not an option. If something broke, you fixed it. That ethos still lingered in him, even when he had started to reach the age where the decades began to blur together.

Although he'd only met her a few minutes before, Luke had read Claudia's file extensively and thought that he knew her well. She was a very different person to what he'd expected, but it seemed to him that she would provide them with exactly what they needed most – new blood to revitalize his clan.

"Is there a problem?"

The young woman's voice suddenly interrupted his

reverie. Luke blinked owlishly, and realised that he'd been caught staring again – twice in the span of as many minutes.

"Hardly." Suddenly embarrassed, he dragged his gaze away. "I was just thinking that it'll be nice to not be the youngest person in the office anymore."

Even though it was true, her expression said that she didn't believe him. She raised one sculpted brow and regarded him coolly, then cut right to the heart of the matter with a single stroke. "Really? Is that why you're ogling me like a randy young choir boy?"

Oh, but she was bold! Luke muffled a snort of laughter behind a cough and tried hard to hide his amusement. Certainly, the ladies of the Immortelle were bold as well, but not in the same way. They tended to be acidic and vicious, and used their wit to burn and belittle. This girl, though - he could feel the sense of humour behind her words even when she was poking fun at him. To his surprise, he found he wasn't offended by it, but actually rather enjoyed it.

"I would hardly call it ogling," he replied, giving her a debonair smile. "Admiring, perhaps. Please do not be offended, I just find you... refreshing." With a flick of his wrist, he distracted her by pointing her towards door of an office nearby. "And this is yours."

"Ah..." Her expression shifted, and her eyes lit up as she looked out across the space. Her teasing barbs forgotten, she rushed past him and hurried over to the windows to gaze out at the sprawling vista of Auckland that unfolded below them. "Beautiful. 'The City of Sails', indeed."

Luke meandered over to join her, and stared out the window as though seeing the city for the first time. In some ways, he was. He'd been in the country for a few years on assignment for his clan, and yet he'd never really taken the time to study his surroundings. After a century of living around the world, cities all started to look kind of the same.

Now, though, he found himself looking with unexpected interest. He took in the vibrant blue of the sky and the mysterious haze where it met the sparkling blue-green glass of the ocean. The city followed the curve of the harbour in a gentle arc; beyond that, he could see the shimmering gold of distant beaches. Closer at hand, the water was peppered with tiny boats in a hundred different colours – the very boats that gave the city its official moniker.

"Yes, it is an impressive view," he agreed, surprised by his own reaction. As though seeing the world with new eyes, he found himself wondering why he'd never noticed the vista before. Surely it had been there all along, and yet he'd laboured on without ever casting his eye out over the city in which he lived. He found that fact both confusing and intriguing.

"So, who gave up the office with the view for me to move in?" she said, rounding on him. The directness of her question and the hunger for knowledge in her eyes took him by surprise yet again, and forced him to take a moment to consider her question.

"One of the senior legal representatives retired a few months ago," he lied casually, lifting a shoulder in a lazy shrug. "She left the office empty, and you just happen to get lucky."

***

"Retired, hmm?" Claudia stared intently at the dark-haired young man, trying to figure him out. She knew that he was lying. It was written through his body language just as blatantly as if he had been wearing a neon sign on his forehead.

That wasn't to say he was a poor liar, though. He was an extremely good at it. Claudia, however, possessed the unnerving ability to read people like a book. It was a skill that she'd been training in since she was a child, and it had become second nature. She'd noticed it on him from the start; deception practically oozed from his pores.

And yet, she needed to be discreet if she wanted to call him out on it. He was her supervisor, after all.

Claudia turned away from him and rested her hands on the sill of the huge, open window, leaning forward until her nose almost touched the glass. Far below her, the bustle of Queen Street carried on unendingly, oblivious to them both. Behind her, Luke was silent and tense, awaiting her next move.

Somehow, a casual conversation had evolved into a verbal game of chess, player against player, each of them vying for dominance over the other. Although in some ways she had the upper hand, she suspected that he possessed knowledge that she wanted desperately, which made her vulnerable.

The never-ending quest for knowledge had driven her since she was a very small girl. Her ability to ferret out the truth in any situation was another facet of what made her so very good at her job – and it also made her extremely good at hiding the truth when she needed to, because she knew all the clues that she would look for if she were seeking something.

Her instinct told her that he knew something about her quarry. Perhaps he was one of them. They didn't think that she knew about them, but she did. The

Immortelle - another presumptuous and arrogant name. She'd first heard the word when she was a child, while poking around uninvited in her mother's belongings. She wanted to know more.

Who were these mysterious Immortelle? What were they? And even more importantly, how were they relevant to her mother and to the father she'd never met?

The hunt had become an obsession. The more she looked, the harder it was to find reliable information. With every step forward, it felt like she was moving farther and farther away from the truth.

Luke was silent and still, watching her intently. It was her move.

Claudia spoke softly now, gently - casually, even. "I am of the understanding that she died. Suicide, I believe."

Her eyes flicked to him the moment she spoke, and she caught the sudden tension in his chiselled jaw and the narrowing of his eyes before he could hide his emotion. Those tiny signs told her so much more than he intended them to. They told her he was aware of the truth, and hadn't planned on telling her.

"It was all over the news," she said, turning back to the window and staring at the ground far below. She could only just see the spot where the body had landed, on an awning. There was still a dark patch there, either an indentation or blood – she didn't particularly want to know which.

"Yes," Luke said softly, though the tone of his voice told her he was reluctant to talk about it. "But, it's still your lucky break."

"Not hers, though." Claudia pushed herself away from the window and turned to look at him.

She longed to just ask him about the Immortelle and

find out once and for all, but she knew that he would never admit the truth to her willingly. What little she had learned over the years had been hard-won, and ferreted out by subterfuge and stealth rather than direct questions. They were a secretive bunch. They looked just like she did – human – and yet she had learned that some of them could be hundreds or even thousands of years old.

She'd heard so many different names for them in her research. The Immortelle, the Cabal, the Führung in German, even the Illuminati – though she was dubious about the latter. They were a secret society like any other, of that much she was certain, except for one simple fact: this one actually existed. Claudia had come to the decision years ago that her mother was a member, and perhaps her father was as well, but her conclusion had come from overheard conversations and sneakily read emails rather than cold, hard facts.

It was the one secret that she had never been able to extract, and it was the one that drove her mad. Here, her research told her she might finally be able to find answers. Luke Cavenelli could very well be her means to that end.

"No, it wasn't." The young man sighed heavily and shook his head. "I'm sorry, it's just… the suicide is something of a sensitive topic around here at the moment, as I'm sure you can imagine. She was our colleague, and our friend. It took us all by surprise. We had no idea she was depressed at all."

"Of course." Claudia relaxed a little bit when he opened up to her. This time, there was an edge of honesty about his demeanour. "I understand. It must have been very traumatic for all of you."

"Yes." He summoned a faint smile for her benefit,

but she could see the tension behind his eyes and knew instinctively that she'd touched on a raw nerve. To her surprise, she found herself wanting to comfort him. Although he had lied to her, there was good reason for it and she wasn't completely without sympathy.

"I'll tell you what," she suggested. "Why don't we go out for lunch today, and we can talk? My treat."

She was rewarded by the sight of his expression relaxing a bit, and then he gave her a nod. "That sounds good. There's an excellent sushi restaurant just downstairs."

"Good." She smiled vibrantly, the kind of smile that could light up a room. "Then it's a date."

Chapter Two

Claudia's first weeks at Cornelius Pharmaceuticals passed without incident. On the surface, it appeared to be just like any other job, but the more she waited and bided her time, the more she found herself feeling certain that there was more to the company than met the eye. It was the little things that stood out most to her, like the alarming lack of cake. After nearly a month without a single office birthday party, she snuck a look at the human resources files and discovered that the date listed as William Logan's birthday had passed three days earlier, without a word from him or anyone else. That was hardly evidence that would stand up in a court of law, but it definitely set off alarm bells in the back of her mind.

Still, she couldn't be on the alert constantly or she'd go mad, so she decided that the weekends would be reserved for her own mental health. She spent them reading, exploring the city, and browsing the local real estate listings until she finally found a new home that appealed to her.

The day that she was scheduled to move in dawned perfectly, bright and sunny, the sky a flawless shade of blue with only the lightest dusting of clouds along the horizon. It was a truly beautiful day, the very best kind of Saturday. Claudia had been awake since dawn, bursting with excitement and so very ready to spend a little time nesting.

But, of course, the moving company was late.

She sat in her car, parked on the edge of the street outside of her new house, and battled her annoyance at their tardiness. She only had two days to get settled in before she was back to the office, and she wanted to use that time wisely. The cargo container with her belongings had arrived the week before, so they'd had plenty of time to get ready. There was really no excuse.

She fished out her phone and tried to call them, but their number went straight to voicemail. After three attempts, she left them a scathing message and hauled herself out of her car. At least she could get started on hanging her clothing. She'd been living out of suitcases for the last month and a half in a mid-city hotel, wearing what little she had been able to bring with her on the plane.

Of course, 'what little' to Claudia Bell was 'good lord, that's a lot of clothing' to every other sane human being on the planet. As the only daughter of Antoinette Bell, the CEO of one of the most prestigious law firms in Australasia, money was not an issue. It never had been, and never would be, unless Claudia happened to do something extraordinarily stupid.

She had been raised with the best of everything. The best schools and the best tutors. The best toys when she was young, and the best clothing and accessories as she grew older. As an adult, though, she'd come to understand the value of money even when it was readily available to her. Even though she had a near-unlimited budget, she was usually wise in her spending habits – unless shoes were involved. Shoes were her bane.

She could have afforded a ten bedroom mansion in Remuera if she'd wanted one, but she chose a two bedroom bungalow in Mission Bay instead. It was a little run down and in desperate need of a coat of paint, but she didn't mind because it had character and it was right on the beach. From her back porch, she could watch the waves crashing on the golden sand, and see the ocean birds fighting and diving for fish.

Likewise, she could have bought herself a Ferrari if she'd wanted to. She had briefly considered the option, but logic intervened. What was the point of buying a car that could go that fast when there are speed limits in place everywhere? Instead, she'd leased herself a small Audi coupe. She would have been just as happy with a little Toyota hatchback, but she had to keep up appearances. There were certain things that people just expected from their lawyer: a posh car and an immaculate manicure, were two of them. A lawyer needed to go to a lot of meetings, and give a lot of handshakes in their day-to-day business.

At that moment, no one would have guessed that she was a high-flying, wealthy lawyer. The weekend was her time, so she was dressed down in a pair of dusky grey yoga pants and a plain white t-shirt, with her hair caught up in a messy bun to keep it out of her face. There would be no clients to see her today, nor any colleagues to impress – or so she presumed.

Claudia popped the boot and went around to the rear of the car to start unpacking. She was too busy to notice the sleek black Mercedes-Benz turn onto her street; one of her suitcases had slipped in transit, and no matter which way she tugged it she couldn't get it to come out. She heard the car pull up against the curb behind her, and then the sound of a door opening and closing, but she was too tangled up in her luggage to get a look at who had arrived.

There were footsteps behind her, and then the

warmth of a body beside her. Someone reached past her and grabbed hold of the suitcase's handle, to help her yank the luggage free. With their combined strength, the bag eventually came loose, but it did so suddenly enough that she almost fell over backwards in the process. Again, a strong hand helped her and steadied her until she got her balance back. She shoved a strand of hair back out of her face, and looked up into a pair of twinkling blue eyes: her assistant was none other than Luke Cavenelli himself.

"What are you doing at my house?" she demanded, equal parts alarmed by his unexpected arrival and amused by the serendipity that placed him at her side just when she needed the help. A smile curved his lips and he held up a large brown envelope.

"William asked me to drop this off," he replied. "It's the brief for the meeting on Monday. With all of those last minute amendments, we thought you'd like the chance to take a look at it over the weekend."

"Oh, well – yes, I would. Thank you," she said. She took the envelope from his hand, and automatically turned it over to slip her nail beneath the seal.

Luke lifted a brow and glanced at the pile of luggage around her feet. "Don't you think we should move this inside before you go getting yourself distracted?"

Her hands froze, midway through removing the contract from the envelope.

"Ah... yes, I suppose you're right." Suddenly, she felt a little silly. He'd managed to take her by surprise, and catch her in a rare moment when her guard was down. Then his words sank in and she turned back to stare at him. "Wait—'we'?"

"Well, I'm already here," Luke replied, absently scratched his chin and looking just as uncertain as she felt. "So, you may as well make use of me. Moving house on your own isn't exactly a pleasant experience."

"True," she said, nodding.

Although she felt a little uncomfortable accepting his help, the practical side of her nature won out. An extra set of hands would make the task go quicker, and who knew when the movers were planning to show up? She made up her mind in an instant, then shouldered her purse, tucked the envelope under her arm, and bent down to gather up as many of the smaller pieces of luggage as she could carry. Then, she led the way up the overgrown garden path to the front door of her little cottage.

By the time she got the keys out and unlocked the front door, she could hear the sound of Luke's rough breathing right behind her. She glanced back at him and watched with amusement as he lugged her largest suitcase up the walk with obvious difficulty.

"What in the world have you got in here?" he gasped when he finally reached her. He followed her inside and set the suitcase down on the hardwood floor in the middle of the hall with a sigh of relief, then looked at her expectantly.

"Bricks, mortar, kettlebells and a lot of shoes," she answered without missing a beat, which drew a chuckle from Luke. He went off to go fetch another load, leaving her alone in the entrance of her new home.

The place was small but just right for her needs, with one huge bedroom complete with a walk-in closet, and one smaller bedroom that doubled as a conservatory on the back of the house. The closet was what had sold her, of course; well, that and the view. She went into the bedroom and opened the closet's concertina doors, to stare admiringly into its cavernous depths. Shelves for her shoes lined one entire wall, and the other was adorned with racks for her hanging garments. Although it was less than half the size of her wardrobe at her mother's house, she was thrilled with it because it was hers and hers alone. She went back to fetch her big suitcase and dragged it into her bedroom, then she unzipped it and began the process of carefully unfolding the dry cleaning bags within.

She was half-way through hanging her clothing when Luke returned. He glanced around the big, empty bedroom with a brow raised. "I see that you live a little spartanly."

"I sleep in a suitcase, didn't you hear?" she joked back, and then switched to the truth for a change. "Seriously, though, the movers are an hour late. If they don't get here soon, I'm going to be very, very upset."

"Oh, I think they're outside," he said, gesturing towards the front door. "There was a truck pulling up in the driveway as I came in."

Claudia gasped and ran past him, leaving him to finish his sentence to an empty room.

***

Startled by the sudden movement, Luke hopped back out of the way and watched Claudia scamper off with great amusement. He trailed along after her to watch the organised chaos ensue.

The house she'd picked surprised him. He had imagined her as the sort of person that lived in a modern, mid-city penthouse apartment, much like himself, not out on the beach in a run-down old villa. His nostrils flared to draw in a lungful of the crisp, salty air, and then he looked up to study the deep, blue arc of the sky above him. On closer examination of the facts, it did make sense. She was obviously attracted to the simple beauty of nature in a way that he'd all but forgotten over the decades. That was one of the many things that he found so intriguing about her, and one of the reasons that he'd lied to her as an excuse to see her outside of work. William hadn't asked him to bring her the documents at all; he'd both suggested it and volunteered, a way to spend time with her outside of the office and the constant supervision of the Cabal.

Over the last few weeks, he'd found himself becoming fond of the pretty young lawyer, but getting close to her was difficult due to the restrictions of Cabal politics. Given the choice, he would have simply asked her out on a date, but that was not his decision to make. The Cabal hadn't given him leave to pursue a relationship with her just yet, and until they did his hands were officially tied.

Then at lunch on Friday, she'd mentioned that she was going to move house that weekend, which had provided him with the perfect opportunity. He had discreetly delayed the final draft of the documents until after she'd left for the day, to give himself an excuse to stop by. Once he was there, logic said that he might as well stay and help her. It was the gentlemanly thing to do.

He wondered if she would be angry if she knew the real reason he'd come to visit, or if she'd be flattered and reciprocate his interest. Over the seven weeks that she'd been working at *Cornelius*, he'd detected signals that indicated she might be attracted to him, but it was so hard to tell if the flirtation was real or merely an unconscious reaction to his supernatural abilities.

Luke lingered through the bustle of the movers, leaning against the porch railing where he was out of their way. Box after box emerged from the back of the truck, lugged by burly men in stubby shorts and grubby t-shirts. Then, out came the furniture, wrapped in heavy plastic to protect it from the rigors of intercontinental travel. Claudia took command, and guided them with the persuasive power of a general directing a battle. He found it fascinating that, despite her relatively small size, she had no problem ordering about men that towered over her.

Almost as quickly as it had begun, the flurry of activity was over. The furniture was arranged, the movers were paid, and the truck reversed down the driveway to leave just the two of them behind. Claudia turned to re-enter her new home, only to freeze when she suddenly seemed to realise that Luke was waiting on the porch.

"You're still here," she pointed out, eyeing him warily. "Don't you have anything better to do?"

He was taken aback for a moment. Her words stung a little bit, primarily because they were accurate.

"Not really," he admitted. "If I go home, I'll just end up working, or maybe curling up on the couch with a book. Out here, the sun is shining, the birds are singing, and the ocean is sparkling. It seems almost criminal to waste a fine day like this inside, don't you think?"

"You're very peculiar, Mr Cavenelli," she told him in no uncertain terms, and then she breezed past him into the house, leaving him to admire the way her figure looked in her casual outfit. This time, she was too distracted to catch him out, busy rushing around the house getting her essentials unpacked. He followed her and allowed himself to be directed towards the kitchen, where boxes of crockery and cookware waited to be put away. As he stepped through the archway into the light, airy kitchen, he found himself feeling surprisingly content with his lot.

It had been a long time since he'd done something so simple, so grounded, so… human. He couldn't even remember the last time he'd moved house by himself. People like him had servants to do all their mundane tasks, though they called themselves different names in modern times. Maids, personal assistants, interior decorators. Whatever the title, it all boiled down to one thing: they were people that did things for him that he couldn't be bothered to do himself, in exchange for a tiny fraction of his substantial fortune.

Here, though, it felt different. Comforting. Even though it wasn't his home, he felt pleasantly at ease and he enjoyed the simple task of stacking row upon row of glasses and plates neatly into the cupboards. One of the mugs was out of line, so he paused to adjust it and set it straight beside its fellows. As the cupboard filled, he felt an inordinate sense of pride completely out of proportion to the size of the task.

Eventually, the box was empty and he went off in search of another. As he walked back into the dining room, a small but heavy carton almost tripped him. He knelt down to pick it up, and read the label: 'Study'. By the weight of it, it presumed that it contained books. Seeking a repeat of the pleasantly domesticated feeling he had encountered a moment before, he picked up a box-cutter and slit the tape.

What he found inside was the last thing that he expected to find, and it blew his good mood completely out of the water.

Sure enough, inside the box was a neat rows of books. That in itself was not unusual, but what did surprise him was the subject matter of the books themselves. They were replicas of old titles that dated as far back as the Inquisition – and he knew each and every one of them, because they were in some way linked to his people.

Luke froze and shot a glance back over his shoulder, concerned that he might be caught. In another room, he could hear Claudia's movements and her faint, happy humming as she sorted through her extensive closet. He had some time then. She'd be busy for a while. The thought brought him no amusement.

He picked up the first book, and turned it over to examine the spine, then he opened it to examine the forbidden text. Perhaps it was just a misunderstanding. Perhaps someone had slipped the box into her belongings to frame her. Maybe it wasn't her fault.

A stab of dread clutched at his heart when he discovered a faint pencil line beneath the most damning segment, highlighting the entry that was the very reason this book was deemed taboo by the elders of every clan. Worse still were the notes in the margins, written in Claudia's distinctive handwriting.

To protect the Immortelle, the writers of those tomes had been hunted down centuries ago. Instructions had been dispersed amongst the clans to destroy any copies of the books that might ever surface - along with any mortal who read the information they contained. Although the event had taken place centuries before he was born, in the early days of his training the need to destroy that damning literature had been drummed into him with great vigour.

Luke closed the book, drew a soft, deep breath, and let it out slowly to try and calm his racing heart. What he'd found was dangerous, even life-threatening if the others found out that she had them in her possession.

A quick scan of the other books told him what he needed to know: the box was a death sentence as surely as a noose around the neck. Although she was important to their plans, she was not irreplaceable. The Cabal had created her, and they could create a replacement if they desired. Her genetic code was what was important, not her, and they would be patient enough to wait while a clone grew to age if they had to.

Luke found himself suffering a strange conflict of emotions. On one hand, it was his duty to turn her in and to ensure that those damning books were destroyed once and for all. On the other hand, he genuinely liked Claudia Bell, and that was something he hadn't felt in a very long time.

Stealing the books seemed like a peculiar way to show his fondness, and yet it was the only way that he could think of to ensure her safety. He snuck a quick glance into the master bedroom and saw her contentedly arranging her shoes, oblivious to his dilemma. Her back was to him so she wouldn't see him go. It only took a moment for him to decide.

With as much stealth as he could muster, Luke packed the books back into their carton and sealed it up, then snuck out of the house like a thief in the night. She didn't even realise that he was gone until an hour later, when she wandered out to check on his progress. With her house in a shambles and boxes strewn everywhere, she didn't notice the theft straight away.

Left bewildered by Luke's sudden departure without even saying goodbye, Claudia just shrugged and resumed unpacking on her own.

Chapter Three

It was rare for Luke to feel anything that resembled real human emotion anymore. After all, he'd been practicing law for the better part of seventy years. Without the emotional stimuli of family and friends to keep his mind active, immortality would eventually begin to dull his perceptions and turn him into a hollow, unfeeling shell, just like it had for so many of the others.

But, the drudgery of eternity had not destroyed all of his humanity just yet.

When Monday morning rolled around, he found himself unable to face the thought of seeing Claudia in the office. How could he casually chat to her about work-related nonsense while knowing that he'd stolen from her? He couldn't bring himself to face her, so he chose to do something that he hadn't done in a very long time: he took a personal day.

The books were already destroyed, reduced to ashes in a little fire pit somewhere along that lovely beach. He had felt a strange compulsion to destroy them quickly and quietly, without letting anyone else see, but he couldn't figure out why. It had been so long since he'd felt anything towards anyone that the whole situation confused him.

In the years since he'd taken the elixir, his entire biology had changed. He barely slept anymore, just a few hours each night. Time and disease could not touch him. He still ate, but his diet had changed. He had become more carnivore than omnivore, preferring protein-rich meats and cheeses over fruits and vegetables. Although his body could still process plant matter, it seemed to have no impact on his health one way or another.

Alcohol, however, was not an option. Once, he had tried to drink a glass of wine at a function. The effects had hit him like a sledgehammer, and after a single glass he could barely walk straight. That was seven decades ago. He hadn't touched a drop since.

Today, he was sorely tempted to drink himself into oblivion anyway.

Luke heaved a deep-throated sigh and rubbed one hand across his forehead. His laptop sat open in front of him but it failed to hold his interest. Today, for the first time in a very long time, Luke suffered the peculiar sensation of guilt. He didn't much care for the feeling, and yet no amount of cajoling or distraction would make the gut-curdling sensation go away.

There was an email from Claudia in his inbox. Every time he went to open it, he found himself making excuses not to. Half a day later, it was still sitting there unopened.

We're colleagues, he tried to remind himself. *It's probably just some stupid get-well-soon ecard.*

His inner voice was not convinced. She did not strike him as the kind of person to send ecards. Cursing himself for a coward, Luke tore himself away from the laptop and retreated to the bathroom to drown his sorrows beneath a deluge of hot water.

A few minutes later, he stood slumped beneath the steaming shower with his head resting against the wall, letting his thoughts drift at random. Inevitably, they made their way back to Claudia. The curve of her hips beneath those svelte skirts she wore, the swell of her bosom, and the delicate scent of her perfume...

In that moment when he'd bent over her to help her get her suitcase out of the car, he'd caught a whiff of her fragrance. It lingered with him in the back of his mind even now.

With a jolt, he realised his body was responding to the thought of her with more intensity than he'd felt in years. He muttered a curse beneath his breath, and swung the thermostat hard to the right, to turn the stream of water ice cold.

***

By the time he'd cooled himself off and returned to the computer, a second unread email had joined the first. This one was from William Logan. Luke stared at it for a long time, and concern added its distinctive flavour to the twisting in his gut.

Had Mr Logan found out about what he'd done somehow? But he'd been so careful to make sure that no one had seen him. He dreaded the thought that this email condemned that lovely young woman to death, before he had the opportunity to explore these strange new sensations that she was stirring in him.

Her name was the subject line.

Mr Logan would know if he failed to read the email in a timely fashion. The Immortelle controlled the world, and there was far more to their empire than just pharmaceuticals. He had no choice but to read it, so he swallowed his feeling of dread, clicked the link, and quickly read the contents.

Lucio,

We've reached an agreement. You are to commence your part of the operation immediately. I have ordered her to visit your apartment this evening. You know what to do.

- Logan

Luke stared at the email, and read it through three or four times before the words finally sank in. His stomach dropped to his knees. What he was expected to do was quite possibly the worst thing for him to try in his current state of mind.

He was supposed to seduce her.

Well, at least you don't have to kill her, the perverse little voice in the back of his head commented. *Not yet, anyway.*

***

Seduction was the last thing on Luke's mind as he aimlessly paced his apartment like a caged animal, trying to think of ways to avoid doing what he was supposed to do. As much as he found Claudia fascinating, he knew that it wouldn't take her long to figure out what he'd done when she realised that her books were missing, and then she'd be furious.

If she already knew, then she was unlikely to be receptive to the idea of sleeping with him. If she didn't, then he might stand a chance of coaxing her into his bed, but he wouldn't be able to live with himself afterwards.

"Christ, why don't I just use the Power on her like everyone else?" he complained to the empty room, but he already knew the answer to that question. Luke found the thought of using his abilities against a helpless mortal deeply repugnant, and tantamount to rape.

As a member of the Cabal's bloodlines, Luke's flesh came equipped with a potent arsenal of biological tricks. He held in his hands the ability to make women writhe in desire at the lightest touch, or to enjoy the kind of earth-shattering orgasms that most only dreamt about. Many of his brethren used their power wantonly, without the slightest regard for their victims, but Luke was not like most members of the Cabal.

Unfortunately, the very same moralistic difference that set him apart from his brothers and sisters made the dilemma that he faced so much harder. If seducing Claudia was out of the question, then he would have to find a way to delay the inevitable. He could hardly feign illness — Mr Logan knew as well as he did that he couldn't get sick. Ignorance, perhaps? Could he pretend to misinterpret the instructions, and entice her into a lively game of chess instead? No, that wouldn't work either. William Logan had briefed him personally before her arrival. They'd even smiled and joked together about how enjoyable this particular mission was going to be for him.

Back then, it had seemed like a perk of the job. Now, he wasn't so sure.

But it could still be a perk, he thought. His mercurial Cabal biology had been tormenting him with increasingly lascivious daydreams about her. He struggled to control them, but they came more and more frequently; he couldn't even go to the kitchen for a glass of water without being troubled by the image of her nude body bent backwards over that kitchen counter, with those deliciously long legs of hers wrapped around his waist.

And her scent… oh God, her scent.

His nostrils flared instinctively, seeking what wasn't even there. There were many other strange quirks that came along with the gifts, and it was subtly different for each person. For him, it was a heightened sense of smell.

Luke pressed his fingertips to his forehead to try to block the images from his mind, but he was also cursed by the heightened sex drive that plagued most people with Cabal blood. Normally, he satiated his needs on prostitutes or the occasional frivolous girlfriend, but he still considered himself to be a gentleman and tried to keep his indulgences to a minimum. It'd been a few years since the last time he had been with a woman.

Now, he regretted his restraint.

***

Claudia was not pleased about the task that had been dropped at her feet, but Mr Logan had insisted. His performance about how worried he was about Luke was completely over the top, and she was no fool. She knew instinctively that he was up to something.

She wasn't in the best mood to begin with and all the signs said that Luke was most likely the cause of her ire. The night before, she'd turned her house upside down looking for one of her boxes of books, only to come to the conclusion that it had either been lost in the shift - or someone had taken it. There was only one person in the world with both the opportunity, and the motive.

She'd come into the office fully prepared to rake Luke over the coals, only to have him call foul and stay at home. As was appropriate for work colleagues, she'd sent him an email wishing him well, but she'd been seething on the inside as she keyed in the mindless pleasantries. Now, she was expected to check on him and bring him dinner? Make sure he was all right? If he'd taken her books, then 'all right' was the last thing he'd be.

Acquiring those books had taken some very intense and delicate negotiations, and it had cost her a great deal of money – money that had been very difficult to pilfer without being caught. Replacing them would be next to impossible. Needless to say, she was furious at the thought that Luke might have taken them, after she'd trusted him enough to invite him into her home.

They'd been working together for nearly two months, and in that time he'd always treated her with warmth and respect. She even considered him something of a friend, despite her suspicions that he was one of the Immortelle. Although her research into their society had revealed the usual sinister overtones, she'd come to the conclusion that there was no real basis to it and there was no reason to consider Luke a threat. Or so she'd thought.

She had to admit that she found his ready smile and quick sense of humour very attractive. He was charmingly well-mannered, self-confident, educated, and well-read – all traits that appealed to her. Under different circumstances, she might have even considered striking up a fling with him. The idea of a saucy office romance with a handsome Italian appealed to the sensual side of her nature, despite her mother's best attempts to teach her an objective attitude towards the opposite sex.

According to her mother, men were to be hired, used as necessary, even treated as friends, but never, ever loved. Although Antoinette considered casual sex a perfectly acceptable recreational activity, she'd always tried to teach Claudia not to let her heart get involved.

Of course, Claudia found her mother's opinions on romance peculiar and strangely reptilian, but she could only assume that it must have had something to do with her absentee father. Like any healthy young woman, Claudia enjoyed her fantasies and kept her own opinions on love and sex. She enjoyed romantic fiction a great deal, but at just 26 years of age she was still trying to figure out what she really wanted from her own relationships in the long term. Whatever it was, she was fairly certain it didn't involve treating men as disposable sex toys.

Still, she enjoyed a good fling as much as the next girl. Luke radiated a certain suave charm that she found fascinating. He wasn't greasy and creepy like so many other men in her line of work, but genuinely polite and respectful. For lack of a better word, he behaved like a gentleman. It was a peculiar, old-fashioned kind of attitude that she'd never encountered before, but she liked it a lot.

He treated her not only as an equal, but as a lady as well. When they went out to lunch together, he opened doors for her and insisted she be served before him. At first, Claudia had been startled by his behaviour, but it had grown on her when she'd come to realise that he wasn't trying to impress her or make a pass at her. It was just his way. He was never even remotely condescending towards her, but always courteous and genuinely interested to hear what she had to say.

She'd come to really enjoy spending time with him, and that made the betrayal hurt all the more.

The address that William had given her was an inner city apartment block only a few streets away from the office, so she left her car in the parking garage and walked. The early evening air was refreshingly cool after the heat of a midsummer day, but it did little to cool her temper.

She walked swiftly, her heels click-clacking across the pavement as she wove in and out of the pedestrian foot traffic. Although she drew the usual admiring stares, it was mostly from women tonight, since she always wore her favourite pair of blood red Jimmy Choo heels when she was in a foul mood. For once, she didn't enjoy those envious stares at all.

Claudia stopped briefly to pick up a few packets of sushi from a vendor open late to attract the dinner crowd, but then she was off again. The longer she waited for the confrontation to come, the angrier she'd be. With as much self-control as she could muster, she buried her rage deep down inside. After all, he could still be innocent. If she bit his head off and he turned out to be blameless, then not only would she feel like an idiot but she'd have put her job at risk, and with it her investigation into the Immortelle.

Adjusting her purse with an irritable jerk, she mounted the half-dozen steps to the lobby of the apartment building. There was a security guard in the doorway, but she blazed past him without even stopping to look. He glanced at her but didn't bat an eyelid. With her expensive clothing and immaculate grooming, she looked just like one of the usual residents that he saw come and go every day.

The elevator swished open with the soft tinkling of Muzak. William had given her an access key that let her into the secure elevator, so she swiped herself in and rode it all the way up to the penthouse. There, she was forced to knock on the door and wait for several minutes. With every passing second, her irritation grew. Despite that, she swallowed her emotions and hid them behind an implacable mask, just the way she'd been taught.

Eventually, the door opened and Luke stood there, staring at her. His bright blue eyes seemed to have somehow faded to grey. The guilt was written clearly across his face as clearly as if he'd taken a permanent marker to his forehead. He turned away without a word, allowing her access to his home without actually inviting her in.

Claudia took the invitation anyway. She stepped through the door, closed it behind her, and let the lock click back into place. With a swift glance around, she assessed the apartment and judged it nice but austere. To her left, an open plan kitchen faced out over a huge, airy living space that was bigger than her entire house. Off to one side she saw a doorway that led to a bedroom, and another that was closed so she could not see where it led. Although the ro74oms were enormous, the furnishings were sparse and the apartment looked strangely barren. There was no sign of her books anywhere.

Luke retreated to the couch while she orientated herself. He looked terrible, she realised suddenly, with his eyes all sunken and his lips set in a deep frown. Her rage wavered for a moment, but she bolstered it back up with determination.

That man had stolen from her, she was sure of it. He'd taken away her only means of finding out who – or what – her father really was. She would not forgive him so easily.

She set her purse and the sushi down on the breakfast bar, and crossed the room towards him with a determined stride. He glanced up as she moved and seemed to shrink within himself, but there was nowhere for him to hide. Claudia planted her hands on her hips, and fixed him with an icy stare.

"Did you take them?" she demanded, her voice practically crackling with frost. He gave her a brief, plaintive look, but he couldn't hold her gaze for more than a few seconds before dropping his eyes back to the floor. His body language said he was guilty long before his shoulders sagged and he finally gave her a nod.

"I'm sorry," he said softly. He ran his hand back through his hair and ruffled it messily, his voice little more than a murmur. There was no guile in him now, none of his lawyer's tricks; his own sense of remorse had stripped it all away, and left him laid bare before her fury.

Luckily for him, his apology and his body language made her hesitate, and her anger began to waver. For all her training, she was still young and her emotions boiled close to the surface.

"Why?" she demanded, glaring at him. "They're not worth anything, and you clearly don't need to steal for a living. Just give them back and we'll forget this ever happened."

"I can't." He looked up at her again, his eyes sad and yet appealing. They just stared at one another for what felt like forever, each willing the other to break first. In the end, he lost the battle. His shoulders slumped again, and he looked down at his feet. "I had to burn them. Truly, I'm sorry. There was no choice."

"What?!" Claudia exploded, her anger so intense that he flinched. "Why in God's name would you burn my books? Do you have any idea how hard it was to find those?" Her voice broke, and she choked back tears of despair. "I haven't done anything to hurt you. Why would you do this to me?"

All the years of training drained away as hopelessness

flooded through her. Ten years of research, of hard study and endless months spent digging through bookstores, libraries, and the internet - all gone. A sob tried to break past her defences, and she couldn't fight it back. She just gave in to them, buried her face in her hands, and cried.

***

Luke leapt to his feet and wrapped his arms around her shaking body, in a hopeless attempt to comfort her. It didn't work, but he was compelled to try nevertheless. He'd forgotten how horrible it felt to watch a woman cry – worse, to make a woman cry. It was like a knife in the gut to see the distress he'd caused in someone so young and beautiful. It was more than he could bear.

"I'm sorry, Claudia – I had to," he admitted. He held her close and whispered in her ear as she wept on his shoulder. "Those were forbidden books. If anyone else had seen you with them, then you would have been executed." His voice dropped lower, almost to a whisper. "I should have killed you on Saturday, the moment I found out that you had them, but... I couldn't do it."

She shoved him back then and stared up at him, her mascara smeared ever so slightly by her tears. Rather than marring her beauty, he found her even more attractive for that tiny flaw.

Her words, however, made him flinch.

"You *are* one of them!" she hissed. "I knew it! You and Mr Logan, you're both—"

"Don't!" he interrupted her, and silenced her by pressing a finger against her glossy crimson lips. "Please, don't say it. Knowing anything about us without permission puts your life at risk – and I'm risking mine by trying to warn you away."

"Why?" she whispered back, staring up at him with turquoise eyes that suddenly seemed so enormous and vulnerable. "I don't want to hurt anyone, I just—"

"'Nothing is true, everything is permitted'," he recited the quotation softly, and reached up to run tender fingertips through the pristinely coifed hair at her temples. The curls felt so silky beneath his touch that he could scarcely believe that they were real.

And her scent, so close, so sweet...

He wanted her so badly, but couldn't bring himself to do it. Even though he possessed the ability to make her do anything he wanted, he couldn't convince himself to abuse the Power like that – or to abuse her like that. While she was still struggling to comprehend the scope of his words, he gathered the Power around him in a completely different way. As gently as a father wrapping a newborn baby in a shawl, he enveloped her in his Power and embraced her with it.

He felt her gasp and struggle within his arms, but only for a moment. Although she resisted his will as well as any of her breeding could, she'd not yet tasted of the elixir and she was still mortal. She could not hold her own against him for long.

Luke caught her as she slumped unconscious in his arms, and held her gently. With as much respect as he could, he carried her to his bed and placed her between the sheets, removing only her shoes and jacket to allow her modesty to remain intact.

Then he stood back and watched her, even more conflicted than before. Some of the elders had the ability to erase memories, but he was not that skilled yet. Luke was still young by their standards, two years shy of a century. He lacked the ability or the skill to fix what he had wrought.

He didn't know what to do.

Chapter Four

Claudia slept deeply that night, in a state that was more like a coma than anything natural. No dreams danced through her mind, and even unconscious she was bewildered by the strangeness of it all. Normally, she enjoyed her dreams and looked forward to that time when her imagination could run wild, but tonight she felt trapped within her own skin. Occasionally, a snippet of memory would drift through her mind: a flash of blue eyes, the feel of a hand upon her skin, or a faint whiff of cologne. They were unusual, half-realised fantasies, but nothing coherent enough to really be called a dream.

It was dark when she finally came awake, but the haze of confusion still hung over her. The bed didn't feel like her own, but she couldn't remember going anywhere else. It took time before her memory began to return, and she began to slowly piece together what had happened the night before.

The tears returned unbidden when she remembered that her precious books were gone, but she was alone this time and could grieve in peace. She cried silently for a few minutes, until the grief faded and left her feeling wrung out but clear-headed.

A clock glowed on the bedside table, advising her that it was just after four in the morning. She'd slept for about eight hours, and yet she didn't feel refreshed at all. Her recollection of how she'd fallen asleep was vague. She knew that Luke had done something to her, but she wasn't sure what.

She wondered if he'd drugged her, but in her heart she knew that wasn't the case. What he'd done was inadvertently show her that he wasn't human, which both validated her theories and made her worry. How could she fight someone with that kind of power? She had no idea what he was capable of.

But he hadn't hurt her at all, even while she was at his mercy. What was it that he'd said? That he was supposed to kill her, because of the books? But he hadn't killed her – in his own words, he couldn't do it. He'd even given her some of the information she craved, in the form of vague half-truths that raised more questions than they answered. Surely he'd known that his cryptic words would only make her search harder. He *must* have known that. Was he just toying with her?

Claudia eased herself out of the bed and looked around in the semi-darkness. Her shoes were on the floor, and her jacket was draped over one of the bedside tables. She picked them both up, and rose to her feet. There was no sign of Luke in the bedroom, but a faint light shone through the doorway from the living quarters. She peeked through, and spotted him reclining on the couch, reading off the glowing screen of a tablet.

He was well away from the door and his back was to her, so she could probably sneak past him if she wanted to. Her purse was still on the breakfast bar, so she could fetch it along the way.

But, if she snuck out then, she would have a great deal of difficulty squeezing him for answers. Here, in his home territory, he was more vulnerable and more liable to give away snippets of information. She sensed that

Mr Logan was his superior in more ways than one; the risk of questioning him at the office would put them both in danger. This was her chance to have him alone. She would be a fool to pass it up.

Curiosity got the better of her, in spite of the risks. She set her jacket and shoes down on a side table and ran her fingers through her hair. Without the proper tools to fix her hair, her appearance was simply unsalvageable. Her makeup was probably a mess, too. Nothing she could do about that now, so she'd have to be content with the fact that the just-rolled-out-of-bed look was very *en vogue*. Claudia straightened her shoulders, adjusted her clothes, and then she walked over to him on stocking-clad feet. He started in surprise and watched with wide eyes as she walked past him, and sat down in an armchair nearby.

"You're awake." He sounded confused, as if he hadn't expected her to be awake so soon. He slowly sat up, but seemed to be at a loss for what else to say.

She stared right back at him, and took in his rumpled appearance. His hair was ruffled, a day's worth of stubble darkened his jaw, and he was dressed only in a pair of silky pyjamas with the top hanging unbuttoned over his shoulders. It left the expanse of his chest and stomach exposed, revealing lean, chiselled musculature adorned with only the slightest dusting of dark curls.

It was almost enough to make her forget that he could be thousands of years old. Almost, but not quite.

"So." She pushed aside her attraction and focused on her interrogation. "You're an immortal, and you don't want me to talk about it. Is that correct"?

He sat up a bit straighter, concern dancing across his youthful features. "I'm not quite sure how much clearer I can be then 'they'll kill you if you talk about it', so yes."

"Then it seems logical that you educate me, rather than let me go poking my nose where it's dangerous for us both," she replied, biting the words off crisply, her tone cool and even. Then, she leaned back in her chair and crossed her legs, a gesture designed to make it clear that she wasn't going anywhere until she got what she wanted. "You've already made it clear that you have no intention of killing me, and you know what little information you've given me is unsatisfactory."

"You realise that it could very well cost me *my* life if I talk to you?" he said softly, leaning towards her. His tablet was forgotten, abandoned on the coffee table beside him. She glanced at it briefly, then back at him, assessing the best tactic to use.

Given the way he'd been looking at her ever since they first met, she judged using her feminine wiles to be the most logical course of action. She knew very well how to use her body as yet another weapon in her arsenal if she needed to. Normally she didn't – it made her feel filthy and manipulative – but there was a time and a place for everything. Besides, it didn't count as a dirty trick if the flirtation was genuine, did it?

Claudia eased herself out of the armchair and onto the couch beside him, then reached out to touch his wrist. "Only if we're caught."

"Catching people that betray them is what these people are good at," he whispered back to her, his hand closing around hers. He hesitated, staring down at her slim digits as though he expected her to yank them away, then he lifted her hand to his lips and pressed the softest of kisses against it.

To her surprise, Claudia felt a thrill of pleasure run through her whole body as a result of that tiny gesture, and it set her off balance for a moment. She was so distracted that she almost missed his words.

"If you're patient, then you may just find out what you want to know anyway."

She glanced up and focused on him, frowning. "What do you mean? Stop talking in riddles."

"Sorry," he said, with a faint, embarrassed smile. "I'm a lawyer, it's what I do." Then his gaze flicked up and she found herself staring into those hypnotically bright blue eyes. "What I will tell you, though, is that Mr Logan sent you here tonight for a reason. I was... supposed to seduce you. Obviously, I failed."

"Seduce me?" she echoed, staring at him in confusion. "What good would that do?"

His eyes fell to roam her body for a moment, then returned to her face. He heaved a deep sigh of longing, and shook his head and looked away. "I'm supposed to... assess you. It's hard to explain."

"Wait," she held up a hand, staring at him incredulously. "You're supposed to fuck me upside down and sideways to figure out whether I'm worth divulging secret information to?"

"Basically." He shrugged and offered her a sheepish smile. "You don't know what I am, Claudia. You think you do, but you really have no clue. I have the ability to make you want me like you've never wanted anything else in your life. I could pleasure you all night, and you'd never have to worry catching an infection from me, or getting pregnant unless I wanted you to. I am capable of making you feel the kind of ecstasy you never dreamed was possible – and my point is that I could do it with or without your permission. I could manipulate your mind into thinking you want me, but that's the problem. I... I respect you too much to use you like that."

Claudia pursed her lips, fighting back the urge to say

something snippy. She was so close to breaking him, but a sarcastic comment about his prowess as a man wouldn't help things. She'd heard it all before, though in a different context. Immortal or otherwise, men were so precious when it came to their sexuality.

"But how would that help? At least explain that to me," she insisted, leaning in closer to him. He drew back as she did so, but she saw his nostrils flare and noticed the dilation of his pupils. With her free hand, she reached out to touch his thigh, softly trailing her fingertips over the firm muscle hidden beneath a layer of silk. "Please?"

***

Luke was no fool. He knew that she was trying to manipulate him. She was very good at it, and when she flicked those lovely teal eyes up at the end of her appeal, it made his knees go weak. He swallowed hard and tried to remind himself that she was just using him to get what she wanted, but his body had other ideas.

Her scent was intoxicating up this close, though her perfume had faded a bit. Even with her hair messy and her clothing rumpled, she was a beautiful young woman. He longed to touch her, to sweep her up in his arms and carry her away to his bed, to show her the infinite pleasures that only a member of the Cabal could give her.

And yet, he sensed her disbelief. That didn't surprise him. There were some things that only one of the Immortelle could understand, and there were some things unique to the Cabal itself.

The question was, how could he make her understand that without putting her at even greater risk?

***

Claudia watched as he went through internal turmoil, and knew that the flicker in his eyes meant that he was debating whether or not to surrender. She knew that he wasn't stupid and that he was well aware of what she was doing, but she still hesitated for a moment when she realised that the truth was the best means to break his last line of defence. The only problem was, telling him the truth made her vulnerable too.

She made the decision on an impulse, and dropped her gaze to her knees.

"Luke," she spoke his name softly, barely above a whisper. When she lifted her gaze, she found him watching her with the strangest look in his eyes. "I already know more than you think I know."

He stared at her outright, not moving, hardly breathing, his attention completely focused on her.

"I know that my mother is one of you," she said, casting aside the veils of deception at long last. "I've known that since I was a very small child. She doesn't know that I know. All I want – all I've ever wanted – is to know who my father is, or was. She won't tell me anything. Every time I ask she just gives me another lie." Tears welled up unbidden, and there was nothing machinated about them. She sniffed softly and wiped them away with the back of her hand, then lowered her gaze back down to her lap. "Sometimes she tells me that he died in a car accident before I was born. Sometimes she tells me that he left because he didn't want me." She closed her eyes, fighting back a wave of emotion. "Do you know what it's like to grow up thinking your daddy didn't want you?"

A hand touched her shoulder, and when she opened her eyes she found Luke watching her sympathetically. Before he could say anything, she spoke one last time to nail her point home. "I don't care about stealing your people's secrets or exposing you to the world. All I want is to know why my father didn't want me. Is that truly too much to ask?"

"I wish I could tell you." Luke frowned and reached out to her, to gather her up in his arms. In spite of everything, she let him. The truth hurt and she wanted to be comforted. "I really do. I'm sorry."

Claudia sighed softly and leaned against his warm bulk, for once in her life letting real emotion surge through her unabated. She closed her eyes to staunch the flow of tears and focused upon her goal instead. "What about the others? If I pass this... test, would someone tell me then?"

There was a moment of hesitation. She drew back to look up at him, and found uncertainty written across his face.

"Maybe," he said, but he didn't sound sure of himself at all. "I don't know. They might tell you once you're one of us."

Once you're one of us?

She stared at him, but he didn't seem to realise the information he'd accidentally let slip. They wanted to recruit her? To turn her into an Immortelle? That made an evil kind of sense. The job opening, her mother knowing about it before the rest of the world, the swiftness of her recruitment... all the pieces were there.

Despite all of her hard work, she hadn't gotten the job on her own merits at all, but rather because they wanted to assess her and see if she was eligible to join their 'elite brotherhood'. Anger flared up in her heart. It took all of her willpower to fight down the urge to clock poor Luke, but he was just the messenger. An underling, who was trying to do what he was told, but not doing a very good job of it because he seemed to be putting her well-being above his own.

That thought struck her as odd. Then it occurred to her that he might have feelings for her. Although they'd only met recently, who knew how the heart of an immortal works? It seemed impolitic to ask him outright, so she decided to try another tactic.

"So, if I let you seduce me, then there's a chance I may get the information that I want?" she asked him, openly and without guile. To her surprise, he actually flinched.

"Potentially," he said, his gaze flicking away. "But, as I said, I'm not going to seduce you."

"Why not? I know you want to. I'd have to be blind not to see it." Claudia reached up to touch his cheek and tried to turn his face towards hers, but he resisted her touch. He caught her hand and drew it down, to hold it gently against his chest.

"I told you," he replied, his voice tense. "I respect you too much to do that to you."

As she watched him, she felt a familiar sensation rise in her belly, and realised that she was not in the least offended by the thought of enjoying a night with him in the name of the greater good. Perhaps it was the very fact that he was not willing to use his supernatural abilities against her, or perhaps it was the fact that he had always treated her with kindness and respect.

Whatever it was, he was attractive, but she could have had any number of attractive men. This was something different. In spite of what they'd been through together, she realised that she genuinely liked Luke as a person. She'd felt a basic animal attraction to him from the moment they'd met, but she had tried to ignore it. Perhaps she'd been ignoring her instincts for far too long.

"Luke, please look at me," she whispered, inching closer to him. He obeyed, but his expression was one of very obvious discomfort. "What if I *want* you to seduce me? What then?"

"You don't," he answered bluntly, startling her with the unexpectedly harsh tone of his voice. "You just want your information. You just want to use me, like all the others."

He rose suddenly and abandoned her on the couch. The warmth where he had been lingered for only a moment longer, and when it faded it left her feeling chilled.

He walked away from her, but he may as well have been nude for what little those pyjamas hid. She could see his arousal, and yet he still possessed the strength to reject her. He stopped and stood by the windows that looked out over the twinkling lights of the city, and pretended to ignore her. Even without being able to see his face, she could sense the hurt and anger in his posture and realised that she'd misjudged him.

For once in her life, was Claudia left unsure what to do. She'd finally come to the decision that she did want to share herself with the strange, handsome immortal, and yet he'd chosen to abandon her in the moment when she was most vulnerable. There was something going on that she didn't understand, some aspect of his past that tormented him. She wondered at it, but doubted that she could get him to open up to her so soon.

This, though. This was a misunderstanding, she realised. She just needed to smooth it over, and to help him understand her motives.

"I don't know much about you, and I don't know what kind of girls you're used to being around," she started softly, letting her voice build slowly towards the crescendo. "But I am not a whore, Luke. I choose my lovers carefully, based on criteria that goes far beyond whether I can get information out of them. I offered because I like you, and because I thought it would help both of us. But, if that's how little you think of me, then I guess I should just go."

Claudia rose from the couch and headed towards the door. Before she could get a half a dozen steps, she heard him call her name.

"Claudia - wait, please."

She glanced over her shoulder and found him approaching her. When he reached her, his hands rose to touch her shoulders, but there was still that uncertainty etched on his face. So she waited, and let him sort through his thoughts rather than interrupting. This was not a courtroom, after all, not a time when she needed to push and push until he broke. Romance was different. It required both patience and understanding.

"I'm sorry," he said at last, his hands resting gently on her shoulders. "I didn't mean to imply that you were a whore." He looked away briefly and then back to her, and she could see the pain etched on his face. "I just— I often find that women try to take advantage of me, because I'm young and I'm not very good at controlling myself yet."

There was more to it than that, she sensed, but it was information that required a deeper knowledge of his species to comprehend. While she did know a lot, she didn't know everything yet. There was clearly much more to it that she needed to explore.

"I was wondering why you were so upset with me," she replied, reaching up to rest one hand on his broad chest. "You're expected to do this, though – aren't you? Mr Logan expects it?"

"And the others," Luke replied, nodding. "But I don't want to use you, any more than I want to be used myself. This just seems like such a lose/lose situation."

"You're just looking at it from the wrong perspective," she said, bestowing him with her warm smile. She understood what it was like to have to do things you didn't want to just because it was expected of you. This wasn't quite the same thing, but she could still sympathise.

"I am attracted to you, Luke," she told him softly, almost shyly. "Quite a lot, in fact. To be honest with you, I was thinking about approaching you anyway, before all this nonsense got in the way. So, why don't we forget about them and just do this for us?" She reached out and trailed a finger across his belly. "You do like me, don't you?"

She felt him suck in a deep breath at her touch, and when she glanced up at his face again she found him watching her with longing. He nodded slowly when she caught his eye, as though admitting something embarrassing. "I do, and I do desire you."

"I promise not to take advantage of you," she whispered, running her hand across his stomach, admiring the smooth musculature. She felt his breath quicken at her touch, then his hand rose to cup her cheek, his thumb trailing along the curve of her jaw.

As though a dam had been broken between them, he swooped down and captured her in a kiss, placing his arms around her waist to support her. It was a good thing that he did, because to Claudia it was more than just a simple kiss. The touch of his lips set off an explosion of pleasure all through her body, with such intensity that it left her weak at the knees.

It lasted only for a second before he pulled back and

looked down at her, with an expression of concern on his face. "Are you all right?"

"What was that?" she gasped, shocked and a little dizzy from the potency of the sensation.

"As I said, we have certain skills, and, ah, some of them I have less control over than others do," he admitted, looking sheepish. "I'm not very experienced yet, relatively speaking."

"Wow." It was the only thing she could think of to say. A flicker of worry passed through her thoughts, but only for a moment – it was swiftly overwhelmed by the part of her that was fascinated. She had tasted the kiss of an immortal, and it was like nothing she'd ever experienced before.

She wanted another one.

Inhibition fled in the face of such an overwhelming sensation, so she threw her arms around his neck and leaned up to kiss him again. A quick, hard, hot kiss, yet the touch of his skin still set her nerve endings on fire and sent tingles of pleasure all the way down her back with such intensity that left her feeling dazed and aroused. His arms tightened around her and held her against him as he returned her kisses, and lost himself to the heat of rising lust.

She surrendered her will to his hands and let him guide her back to the couch again. Their lips parted as he leaned her back to rest upon the cool leather, but the echoes of the mystically-induced pleasure still lingered. His mouth shifted lower, to the softest hollow of her throat, lavishing kisses and nibbles on her skin; each touch sent white-hot arrows of ecstasy all the way through her, which left her gasping.

He undid the buttons of her blouse and opened it, revealing the lacy underthings that she wore beneath. She felt him shift at the sight of it, and heard his deep-throated groan as he buried his face between her breasts. His hands shook as he tried to remove her bra, and it took him a few attempts before the fabric finally came free.

He wrapped his arms around her and lifted her just enough to strip the garments away, leaving her nude above the waist. Her breathing came in heavy gasps as he touched her and ran his hands softly over the curves of her breasts. Then he kissed them, tenderly, and wrapped his lips around her swollen nipple. The pleasure was so intense that it felt impossible, artificial and somehow unreal, yet it was so overwhelming that she felt her back arch and heard the sound of her own cry echo in her ears.

Then his hands were beneath her skirt, making her quiver as they explored the length of her inner thigh. She expected him to peel the fabric off her and leave her naked, but he didn't. Instead, he inched her skirt up over her thighs until it lay bunched around her waist, exposing her underwear.

She felt his hot breath across her skin as he slid down to place his head between her thighs. His nostrils flared to draw deeply of her feminine scent, and then he slipped a thumb beneath the lace to ease the delicate fabric to one side. She was so aroused that her sex already glistened with its own fluids, even before he leaned in to tease her with the tip of his tongue.

But when he did, it was too much for her. She'd never known such pleasure. It wasn't natural, but she didn't care. The touch of his tongue sent an electric thrill right through her, as if she'd grabbed hold of a live wire. He had her on the brink of orgasm already, and when his tongue slipped within her, she lost control completely.

Her back arched and she tangled her fingers in his

hair, screaming her pleasure without any hope of redemption. It was too late, he had her, there was no escape – she didn't want to escape. Every twist of his nimble tongue sent lightning bolts of pleasure right through every inch of her body, leaving her shivering and exhausted by the time he was done with her.

But, he'd barely even started yet.

She collapsed against the couch as he slid out from between her knees, and crept up along the length of her body to kiss her all over again. She could taste her own juices on his tongue, but she was too distracted to care. His hard, hot body pressed down against hers, trapping her on that couch, and all she could think of was how badly she wanted his swollen cock inside her.

No, not wanted. Needed.

When he broke the kiss and looked down at her, she was writhing like a wild thing beneath him. Her nails dug into his skin, but he didn't seem bothered by the pain in the least.

"Are you sure you're all right?" His voice was a deep-throated whisper, but Claudia didn't have the ability to answer him coherently. His power was potent and overwhelming; she had tasted the barest fraction of it and she was still hungry for more.

Oh, God, how she wanted more.

She wrapped her arms around his shoulders and pulled him down atop her by way of an answer, and he came to her willingly. One of his hands ran up along the side of her waist while the other supported his weight, caressing her tenderly. She wrapped her legs around his waist, her thigh-high stockings sliding smoothly, teasingly across his skin.

***

His hand slipped down to run over her thigh, feeling the heat of her skin through the fragile mesh. Ah, but he loved the look and the feel of stockings, and the tiny lacy things that she wore beneath her clothes. He could feel his own control slipping away with every moment, every touch. After going without for so long, his arousal was so intense that it actually hurt.

He needed to sate himself, before he went mad. And there was a beautiful, willing woman below him that genuinely seemed to want him.

It almost seemed too good to be true.

***

She felt him hesitate above her, but it was too much for her. If he made her wait another moment, she felt like she'd explode. So she took the initiative from him without waiting for permission. With a single finger, she caught the waistband of his trousers and slid them down to expose his swollen cock.

Between their bodies, she caught a glimpse of it and her breath caught in her throat. It was big – not painfully so, but certainly bigger than she'd expected. She could feel his breath hot and heavy across her shoulder and knew that he was holding back, trying hard to keep himself in control.

But she didn't want that. She wanted him to take her, to fuck her hard and fast like an animal. She wanted him to fuck her senseless, and to feel the hot explosion of his seed deep within her. In that moment, it was all she could think of, all that she wanted in the whole wide world. She wondered if he was using his powers against her, but she didn't really care anymore.

She reached down between them to capture his cock,

and guide it into her. With her thumb, she twisted the delicate fabric of her underwear to one side again, and plucked it out of the way. Her legs tightened around him and drew his hips closer and closer, until the heat of her waiting sex parted around the head of his cock.

***

Luke muffled a strangled cry against Claudia's shoulder, but there was only so much that one man could take – and that was it. With a twitch of his hips, he was deep inside her. Control was gone completely, and all that it left behind was pure, animal lust. He took her slow and deep, each thrust of his hips taking her fully and completely – not just with his manhood, but his Power as well. The delicate lace of her underwear tickled him as he claimed her, but he didn't mind that any more than he minded the feel of her nails on his back. It all mingled into one gloriously intense moment of exquisite sensation.

And then she climaxed again beneath him, and her mind opened up to him like a rosebud unfolding. In a moment of pure, unrelenting pleasure, he saw everything about her, everything that she was and everything that she could ever be. It was like a fast-running river of thoughts and emotions, and he was drowning in it, struggling to cope with all the sensation and information that hit him all at once.

***

Claudia was lost in the pleasure of climax when she realised that something was wrong. His body had ceased moving, frozen deep within her, and although she could still feel his hot breath against her neck she knew that something was amiss.

"Luke?" she whispered frantically, squirming beneath him to try and get a look at his face, but she couldn't quite see it clearly. What she could see was that his eyes were out of focus, staring off into the middle distance. A few moments later, his gaze suddenly snapped back into focus and he shook his head as though to clear it, leaving her wondering and confused.

"Sorry," he whispered back, his voice breathless, then he kissed her again and sent another jolt of ecstasy careening through her body. Her concern vanished, blown away on the tides of pleasure.

In that moment only the heat of sex mattered.

***

By the time he allowed himself to succumb to his own orgasm, Luke had felt his young lover climax no less than four times. He fought down the sense of self-satisfaction that came with it, since he knew full well that his biology gave him an unfair advantage over any mortal lover, even one as well-bred as Claudia.

He lingered in her arms for a few long minutes after he reached his peak, enjoying the sense of closeness that came along with the afterglow, until he felt her finally begin to relax. With tender kisses to distract her, he extracted himself carefully from her embrace. Her arms slid away as he eased himself back, flopping comfortably across her belly. She was the picture of contentment, barely awake, when he knelt to gather her in his arms and carry her back to his bed.

She snuggled into him as he moved her, her face nestled against the side of his neck. Warm, sweet emotion twisted in his belly as he looked down at her, but he knew what he needed to do – for both their sakes. It was after sunrise now, almost eight o'clock in the morning. Somehow, they'd lost more than three hours of their lives in the pursuit of pure pleasure, but it seemed like a good investment to him.

However, that did mean he was running late for work.

Mr Logan would understand if she wasn't there — he'd ordered this, and he knew as well as anyone what physical intimacy with one of the Cabal could do to an ordinary human being. Luke had no such excuse. As much as he longed to stay at his new lover's side and hold her in his arms while she slept, he couldn't. He must report to his superior before suspicions rose. More importantly, he needed to figure out how to interpret what he'd learned from her mind so that it wouldn't damn them both.

And perhaps, if he was clever enough and persuasive enough, he might save both their lives. Then, he would have time to think about giving her the attention that she truly deserved.

Chapter Five

It felt like it took forever for Luke to get ready and leave. Claudia lay comfortably in bed pretending to be asleep, but like so many elements of their lives, her restful countenance was only an illusion. Her exhaustion was genuine, though. At one point, she found herself thinking that if he didn't hurry up and get out of the shower soon, then she was actually going to pass out.

It took all of her willpower to lay still and breathe slowly and evenly when she heard him return from the bathroom. He moved around the room quietly for a few minutes while he got ready, and then he approached the bed to check on her. Claudia almost gave herself away when she felt gentle fingers run through her hair. A feather-soft kiss alighted on her forehead, and with it came that delightful thrill of pleasure. It sent a shiver down her spine, but to her relief he seemed to assume it was an unconscious reaction.

At last, she heard his footsteps depart. The apartment door opened, and then closed again with a soft click. She lay still for a while longer, just in case he returned, but the only noise in the apartment was the faint ticking of a clock in the kitchen. Claudia opened her eyes and took a good look around. The bedroom was a large one, with huge mirrored windows that looked out over the western half of the city.

And it's a very good thing that they are mirrored, she

thought as she sat up in bed and stretched languidly, the sensual feeling of afterglow lingering throughout her body. There were curtains, but they were wide open. The nearest building was too far away for her to make out any details, but if it hadn't been for the mirrored glass any pervert with a pair of binoculars could have observed their antics.

To her surprise, she felt a little guilty. She hadn't planned to take advantage of Luke's hospitality, but when the opportunity had arisen to take a sneaky look around his apartment, she had to take it. The idea had only occurred to her when she was snuggled up in his arms, on the verge of falling asleep. It'd been painfully difficult to drag herself back from the edge of unconsciousness and keep herself awake while every inch of her body screamed for sleep, yet somehow she succeeded. She could only hope it would prove worthwhile in the end.

For a moment, she was distracted thinking back to the night before. His arms had been so warm and gentle, and yet so strong. Now that he was gone, she missed him. The feeling both fascinated and confused her.

Claudia shook her head to clear the thoughts away, and then hopped out of bed intending to indulge in a quick shower before she investigated what secrets the apartment hid. She made it exactly one step towards the bathroom before her legs gave out, and she plopped down on the rug feeling bewildered.

"Well, I guess I won't be underestimating his prowess as a man anymore," she said to herself, amused. She carefully got back up again, and made her way into the en suite on legs as shaky as those of a new-born lamb.

A few minutes alone with a high-powered massaging shower head left her feeling a whole lot better, not to mention cleaner. When she stepped out and dried herself on a towel, she found herself admiring the austere utility of the room. Like the rest of the apartment, everything was of the highest quality, yet simple and practical.

Aside from a few pieces of art hung around the living room, there was little in the way of personal adornment or ostentatious displays of wealth. She appreciated that, because it reflected her own feelings about her wealth: quality over quantity, and above all practicality. Money was a means to an end, to be spent as necessary to preserve a certain quality of life and advance her personal goals, but nothing more than that.

Of course, the discovery that she had something in common with Luke made her feel even more remorseful. He must have guessed what she'd do if she woke up before he returned to keep an eye on her, and yet he'd left her unattended anyway. Claudia wondered if he was deliberately giving her the opportunity to snoop, or if he was just too distracted to care. Thinking back, he had seemed anxious. It was reasonable to assume that there was more to his anxiety than she understood.

She borrowed a silky bathrobe hanging on the back of the bathroom door and wrapped it around herself. She would change properly later, but right now she felt like time was of the essence.

A quick search revealed nothing of interest in the bathroom. In fact, there wasn't really much of anything. Luke lacked the usual accumulated clutter most people had under their sink, and the medicine cabinet behind the mirror was devoid of the assorted hair products and expired medication that one would usually expect. He owned one tub of hair gel, one comb, a can of unscented antiperspirant, and an electric razor, all lined up neatly on the vanity, but that was it.

Behind the mirror lurked a bottle of expensive aftershave and a few spare bars of soap. Under the sink, there was nothing at all.

Luke lived a very basic existence compared to her. Claudia's bathroom was a perpetual disaster zone of discarded cosmetics, assorted fragrances, and half-a-dozen different kinds of curlers and straighteners. She wasn't sure if it was a quirk of his personality or just one of the benefits of being a man. Regardless, she put everything back where she found it and turned her attention towards his bedroom instead.

Again, she found very little. His wardrobe revealed an assortment of business suits and stylish leather shoes, but there was nothing secretly squirrelled away up the back or hidden in the pockets. The one thing of interest was that many of the suits were obviously cut in styles that had fallen out of fashion decades before she was born. There was even a double-breasted suit and fedora in the style of the post-war era.

She wondered if that was as far back as his adult life went, but it was just as logical to assume that he'd thrown away anything older than that. The fact that he'd kept those old outfits at all was fascinating to her, but she couldn't imagine his reasoning for doing so. Her best guess was nostalgia, the same reason she kept her old school uniform tucked away in the back of her closet. After a moment of thoughtfully fingering the rough broadcloth of the oldest suit, she retreated from the closet to explore the rest of the room.

To her relief, she discovered that his collection of underwear and socks did *not* date back to the post-war era. She gave the contents of his drawers a quick visual inspection, but refrained from touching anything. There were some lines that she wasn't prepared to cross.

Besides, men weren't as likely to hide things behind their knickers as women were.

The bedroom yielded no further information about him, except for the fact that there was a distinct lack of signs that indicated any other women in his life, despite his bachelor lifestyle. No ladies' clothing, no keepsakes, no photographs. Not even a box of condoms. Most of the bachelors she knew tended to have a few trophies left behind by their previous conquests, but Luke had nothing of the sort. Everything was organised, practical, and clean. Even his ties were hung neatly in a small, dedicated cabinet. Beneath each one, a matching tie clip and cufflinks sat waiting. That sight made her smile; his taste in clothing was excellent, and he even had them organised by colour.

Eventually, she left the bedroom and moved on. The living area revealed no secrets, either – it was sparse to the point of being barren. The room was huge and airy, but the only furnishings were a pair of couches, the armchair, and the coffee table arranged in a little nest near the windows. There wasn't even a television.

What about his tablet? she thought suddenly. It was still sitting on the table, waiting for its owner to return. She went over and picked it up, but she couldn't quite bring herself to sit on the couch - the memories were still too raw and fresh. Instead, she wandered over to stand in front of the enormous windows that looked out over the harbour so that she could enjoy the warmth of the morning sun.

She swiftly discovered that there wasn't much on the tablet, except for a vast collection of eBooks. At first she was merely impressed by the sheer volume of his collection. Then, she was amazed when she realised that every single one of them had been read. There were at least a thousand books in a dozen different languages, and his reading history said that he'd completed them all, with the exception of a handful that he only acquired in the last few days.

Claudia lowered the tablet and stared off across the city, thinking over this revelation. He read more languages than she did, apparently. Courtesy of her mother's strict educational regime, she spoke four languages fluently and could read a handful more. He did have more time on his hands, though. There wasn't much else for him to do. She saw no sign that indicated any hobbies, or any family or friends. One of her professors had once said that there were so many books in the world that it would take an eternity to read them all, and Luke actually had an eternity to find out.

None of the books struck her as remotely incriminating, although there were so many it was hard for her to be certain. They spanned a broad range of topics, from classical literature through to art history. She checked for personal documents as well, but there were none. Eventually, she gave up on the tablet, set it back on the table, and resumed exploring. There was one room left, after all.

The second door off the living room had been closed when she arrived, and it was still closed. She tried the handle and found it unlocked. It opened to reveal a spacious room dedicated as a personal office and library. Her breath caught sharply in her throat as she stepped in and stared up at the floor-to-ceiling shelves, each crammed to capacity with hundreds of different books.

The law, the sciences, art, literature, and philosophy, they were all there in some form or another. Claudia stared around, uncertain where to start. It was overwhelming, and reminded her of sneaking through her mother's personal library, which was only slightly smaller. Then she spotted something even more promising: a laptop computer sitting on a huge oak desk in a corner. It was password protected, but if he was as old as he seemed then there was a good chance that he would be less computer savvy than someone of her generation.

The obvious passwords – variations of his name and the word 'immortal' – didn't work, and left her momentarily at a loss. Then a sudden flash of inspiration struck. There was a silly custom number plate on his Mercedes-Benz, which was a hybrid of his proper Italian first name and the brand of the car: *MERCIO*.

It felt a little foolish, but she was all out of other ideas so she decided to try it anyway and keyed in the letters *M-E-R-C-I-O,* all in capitals. The computer chimed its approval, and the login screen faded to be replaced by his desktop.

The laptop was a mess of files, as one would expect for a busy lawyer for a massive, multinational pharmaceuticals firm. There were several still open from the last time he'd been working from home, but when she checked them she found that they were all purely business related and mostly things she was already involved in.

In the corner of the screen, she noticed the blinking icon that told her an email message was waiting. When she clicked it, she was surprised to discover that it was from her. She vaguely recalled sending him a short get-well-soon message the day before, but that felt like forever ago now. He had never opened it.

However, there was a newer one that he had opened, one addressed from William Logan... and her name was the subject line.

Curious, she clicked on it to see what it contained.

Chapter Six

The elevator chimed as it reached the 15th floor. Luke had worked on that level for several years, and usually he felt safe and comfortable there – but not today. Ever since Carienne Du Pont had decided that she could no longer tolerate eternity and flung herself to her death from the building's roof, it just hadn't felt the same. Now, he was a traitor and he felt like an outsider amongst the people that had once been his colleagues.

If that had been the only problem on his plate, it would have been enough. But no, there was also the issue of Claudia Bell. He'd left her sleeping in his apartment, but the moment he stepped outside he wondered if he'd made the right choice. The girl was smart and voraciously curious. If she woke before he returned it could mean trouble, both for the Cabal and for him.

He was already dreading his meeting with Mr Logan. Trying to decide what he was going to tell his superior was the hardest decision of his life. On one hand, he could tell him the truth. Claudia would be hunted down and executed. She would lose her chance to enjoy eternity - and he would miss her.

On the other hand, he could lie. He might succeed for a while, but eventually they were sure to be found out. Then, they would die side by side. The only perk of that situation was that he wouldn't have to grieve for her. Either way, that lovely, vibrant young woman's fate rested in his hands.

If only there was a way to keep everyone alive. Luke sequestered himself in his office to think it over, closing the door behind him. He was a lawyer, wasn't he? It was his job to protect his client, innocent or guilty. Normally, he was very good at his job. So, why was he having so much trouble with it this time?

You just had to go and get emotionally involved, didn't you? he silently accused himself, slumping into the tall leather chair behind his desk. Under normal circumstances, the first person he'd go to in situations like this was William. They'd worked together for decades. If anyone knew him, it was William.

As well he should. William Logan was his biological father, after all.

Part of him simply couldn't believe that he was hiding the situation from his own father. Surely, if he just opened up and admitted the truth then William would find some way to assist. Unfortunately, has father was as loyal to the Cabal as they came. He was one of the oldest of them, part of the circle of elders that acted as advisors to their supreme leader. Two thousand years of loyalty to the Cabal outstripped any familial feelings he might have had towards his only son.

There was a tap on the door and then it opened. Karen, his personal assistant, entered a moment later.

"Good morning, Mr Cavenelli," she greeted him formally, her stiletto heels click-clacking on the tiles as she crossed the room to set a cup of coffee on his desk. The sound of her footsteps brought back memories of Claudia, but the rich aroma of coffee helped to keep them from overwhelming him.

Although Karen was no beauty, she was swift, efficient, and eternally professional. In a moment like this, when his emotions were at war, he appreciated that. He even found himself wondering if he could ask her for help. She was only a mortal, but she might have some kind of advice for him.

Almost a hundred years old, and you still need advice on women? his inner voice chided. *You idiot.*

He stared down into his coffee, feeling glummer by the second. Suddenly, he realised that Karen was talking to him and he hadn't heard a word she said.

Perceptive as always, she trailed off and raised a brow. "Is everything all right, Mr Cavenelli? It looked like you were on another planet for a moment there."

"I was, forgive me." Luke gave her a sheepish smile and shrugged. "I've been having some... girl trouble lately. Please, start again."

She nodded understandingly and smiled. This time he gave her his full attention as she detailed out in exact order his itinerary for the day, and the messages that had been left for him the day before.

Unfortunately, his first meeting of the day was scheduled with William. He couldn't decide if that was a good thing or a bad thing. With his head as scattered as it was, he doubted that he would be able to focus on anything else, anyway. Once she was done, Karen handed him the pile of messages and mail, then click-clacked out to leave him in peace. That should have given him ten minutes to enjoy his coffee and think of what to tell his father.

It *should* have - except William was early.

His only advance warning was when he heard Karen greeting William on her way out. A second later, he was alone in his office with the last person in the world that he wanted to see. William closed the door behind him, then approached Luke's desk and sat down opposite him. It took him all of three seconds to notice that something was amiss.

"You look like hell, son," William said, staring at him intently. "I hope that means you were successful?"

"No, this is just how I always look before my morning coffee," Luke replied, making a feeble attempt at humour. His heart wasn't in it, but William chuckled diligently anyway.

"Then you did coax her into bed," he surmised. "Good. Did you learn anything interesting?"

That was a difficult question. In that moment when she'd succumbed to glorious climax, her mind had been laid bare to him. He'd seen every one of her dreams and aspirations, every quirk of her personality and even her most secret fantasies. For a single, brief moment in time, he'd known everything there was to know about her, but now it was fading away, growing muddled and hard for him to make sense of.

"To tell you the truth, I'm not entirely sure what I'm looking for," he said, staring down into the depths of his coffee cup as though he might find salvation hidden somewhere within it. "She's strong, intelligent, ambitious, and creative – but we already knew these things. It's... to be honest, sir, this whole thing is bothering me. May we talk for a moment before we go into it any further?"

"Of course, son." William lifted a brow, and leaned back in his chair. Many of the Cabal possessed empathic abilities, and his father seemed to sense Luke's disquiet. "You're having second thoughts, aren't you?"

"Yes," Luke admitted, glancing up for a moment to study his father's expression before his eyes dropped his gaze back down to his coffee. "She's a good woman, sir. She deserves better than this. We're manipulating her, when we could just give her a choice. Why can't we just talk to her, and offer her the chance to join us willingly?"

"That's not how these things work, my boy," William replied with a shrug, absently brushing a speck of dust off his immaculately-groomed suit. "You know that as well as I do. The Supreme Elder decided on the plan long before she put it in my care. We can't just go overriding the Supreme Elder, now can we?"

"We don't have to disobey her to make this work," Luke argued, with every ounce of his persuasive powers. "We could talk to her. The Supreme Elder would understand. Wouldn't it be better if Claudia came to us willingly?"

"She doesn't need to." William's white eyebrows lowered over his eyes, and Luke sensed that he was losing the argument. "What Claudia wants is of no consequence. We only need her for her genetic code."

"But it's wrong, Father. It's morally, ethically wrong." Luke shook his head firmly, then set his jaw. "There are other options – better options for all involved. Besides, I don't know what markers to look for to determine if she's suitable or not."

"Oh, don't worry about that." William chuckled again, but this time it was a dark sound that set Luke's nerves on edge. "You're not the one that has to make that determination – you're just supposed to get her memories, which you then give to me, and I pass on to the other elders. We will make the final decision."

Luke's head jerked up. He stared at his father, his eyes wide in surprise. That part he hadn't known about, and the revelation sealed both their fates. If he gave Claudia's memories to his elders, then they would know what she'd done, and what he had as well.

"I-I'm not sure I'm comfortable doing that," he

protested, his voice stammering as he struggled to hide the racing of his heart and the adrenaline thundering through his veins. "I mean, it's just... it's not very respectful to her. It was an intimate moment, for both of us. She's a lady."

William Logan raised a brow and stared at him, as though trying to figure out whether or not Luke was kidding. It didn't take long for him to realise that he wasn't, at which point his expression darkened. "That's not your decision to make, boy."

Luke tried to think of something else to say, but his father didn't give him the chance. The Power surged up without warning, drawn by William's command. It caught him and wrapped itself around him, locking him deep within its embrace. Frozen like prey in the cobra's stare, Luke was trapped and helpless, unable to move as his father closed on him with dread intent. He felt a cold palm on his forehead, and then the Power was inside him, delving deep into his mind.

He tried to fight it but he couldn't – he couldn't even cry out. William Logan was ancient, and far more skilful than he was. The feeling of his mind being probed was a horrible one, like a cold, wet eel slithering through his skull, drinking in its share of his thoughts and his memories. As if living it all again, he saw that beautiful young woman in his arms, heard her words, and saw her incriminate herself once more.

In that moment, he knew he was destined to die.

Then suddenly, there was a moment of vulnerability. His father's guard dropped just the tiniest bit. He was experiencing the moment of climax, feeling the same pleasures that Luke had felt, in a way that was both intrusive and horribly voyeuristic. During that moment, Luke grabbed a portion of the Power for himself and lashed out with as much strength as he could muster.

William stumbled back away from him, briefly stunned by the unexpected ferocity of the attack. His psychic grip weakened just enough for Luke to tear himself free. Instinctively seeking to defend himself, Luke leapt forward and threw out a fist, clipping his father's jaw with a brutal uppercut. The blow caught him squarely, and William crumpled to the ground.

Luke leapt over him as he fell and ran for the door without any regard for secrecy. Karen's head jerked up in surprise when the door burst open, but he'd already raced past her and vanished down the hall before she could say a word. He dashed through the corridors as fast as he could go, dodging around people and objects that threatened to trip him. A mere physical blow wouldn't keep his father down for long; when he recovered, Luke's life would be forfeit and so would Claudia's. He only had a matter of minutes to get to her, and get her away.

The elevator pinged open just as he arrived in the lobby. He dove straight in, bowling the stunned visitors out of the way. The moment they were gone, he thumbed the button down to the ground floor, and then slumped against the mirrored wall. William was right, he did look like hell – but right now that was the least of his concerns.

For the moment, he had a head start, and if he wanted to save Claudia then he needed to use it. Once William woke up, he would summon the clan's forces. The Cabal was the least militant of the Immortelle clans, but it still had an army, and its army was just as lethal as any of the others. The first place they would check would be Luke's apartment.

The elevator doors slid open on the ground floor,

and he was off again at top speed. The automatic sliding doors in the lobby barely opened in time for him to race through them, but he made it and pelted out into the busy streets, dodging pedestrians and tourists. It was only about mid-morning, so people were everywhere: pushing strollers, shopping, enjoying chats with friends. Every single one of them stopped and stared at the sight of a young man in a thousand dollar business suit tearing down Queen Street as if all the hounds of hell were on his tail.

At the lobby of his apartment building, the security guard tried to stop him to see what was wrong but he waved the man off and hurried past. There was no time to talk, no time to think - he had to get Claudia and get out of there before his father mobilized the troops. A rudimentary plan was beginning to form in his mind, but for it to stand a chance then he needed to maintain their head start. There was information he'd withheld from Claudia to protect her, but now that very same information might be able to save her life.

The elevator to the penthouse seemed to take forever, and all the way up he was tormented by horrible images of what would happen if he didn't get to her in time. The day before, he had been bothered by fantasies of her supple young body in lewd, sexual positions, but now it was so much worse. In his mind, his apartment was already plastered with her blood. He would be next, but he didn't care because she was already dead.

He couldn't bear that thought.

After what felt like an eternity, the elevator doors opened onto the top floor. He threw himself out and into the hallway. He got his door open a moment later and barged through, racing into his bedroom to wake her...

...except that she wasn't there.

Luke froze when he saw the bed was empty, and struggled to process the image before he put two and two together. Then, he ducked out of the room and hurried straight to his office, where he found Claudia frantically closing files on his laptop, so he couldn't see what she'd been reading.

Anger surged through him when he realised that she'd taken advantage of his trust. After how much stress he'd gone through, how much personal risk he'd suffered, she still betrayed him.

Then she looked at him and her exquisite turquoise eyes held a mixture of remorse and fear that made his stomach lurch. She could only hold his gaze for a few seconds before her eyes dropped to her lap. It didn't take the Power to tell him that she was afraid of him.

"I-I'm sorry," she stammered, twisting a segment of her bathrobe — *his* bathrobe — between her hands. "I just… I thought, maybe—"

"Get dressed." His words were cold, but even with anger in his heart, he couldn't bear the thought of letting harm come to that lovely young creature. It was his fault, after all. He knew exactly what fabric she was made of, and he'd chosen to leave her alone in his home despite that. He'd brought it on himself.

Later, when they were safe, he would figure out if he could forgive her for violating his trust.

Her shoulders sagged visibly, but she was smart enough to know when she was beaten. She rose from the chair without argument and made her way to the office door, where he stood with his arms crossed blocking her exit.

***

Guilt wasn't something that Claudia experienced often, but now she truly felt ashamed of herself. She looked up into Luke's face as she approached him, and knew without words that she'd hurt him. In spite of all her training, she found herself unable to hold his gaze for long. She could still feel the lingering heat that his passion had left within her, but she knew that she'd damaged the growing bond between them, perhaps irreparably. He stepped back and let her past, his lips set in a hard, angry line.

Claudia assumed she was being evicted from his home. She gathered up her clothing and took it to where her purse waited in the kitchen, where she paused and shot an uncertain glance around; she wasn't sure if she was expected to dress right there or go in the bathroom. Either way, she felt justifiably unwelcome, and doubted he would leave her unsupervised anywhere in his home.

Luke didn't say anything, so she decided to err on the side of caution. She just slipped the bathrobe off her shoulders right there, and let it fall about her feet. Although she could have used the moment to try and manipulate him sexually, the thought of doing so made her feel dirty and a little nauseated. She could feel his eyes on her as she slipped on her bra and blouse, but she kept her back turned to him so there would be no mistaking her intentions.

Her underwear was in no state to be worn, but her mother had taught her from a young age to always be prepared. She always carried a tiny emergency kit inside her purse, which contained an assortment of vital tools. Amongst the other items was a spare pair of underwear in a tiny plastic bag.

After all, girl never knew what was going to happen in life. Today just proved that maxim.

Uncomfortable and a little frightened, she shot a glance back over her shoulder at Luke, only to find that he was no longer watching her at all – he'd wandered over to the window and was staring at the ground far below. He seemed to sense her attention, and shot a glance back over his shoulder at her, his eyes unreadable.

"I suggest that you hurry," he said, his voice deceptively soft. Confusion and hurt twisted in her gut. She couldn't tell if he was angry anymore, and usually his expressions were so easy to read. How could she apologise? She was a lawyer – she never apologised for anything unless it was part of a ploy. Today, her ploys had all run out.

Her confidence wavered, and with it her gaze dropped back to the floor.

Turning her back again, she shimmied into her clean underwear and slipped her skirt over top, zipping it up over her hip. There was no point putting her stockings back on so she didn't bother. She tucked them loose into her purse along with yesterday's underwear, then picked up her heels and slung her purse over her shoulder. She was halfway to the door when a strong hand caught her, sending an electric jolt down her spine.

"We need to leave," Luke said. His voice was sharp, and carried a terrifying urgency. "Right now."

"We?" Claudia stared at him, bewildered.

His answer was to grab her hand and drag her bodily out the front door. Before she even knew what was happening, he'd flung open the door to the fire escape stairs beside the elevator and pushed her through. A second later he was in behind her. The door swung closed just as the elevator pinged open.

She heard the sound of booted feet thundering across on the landing outside, then the sound of men shouting and the breaking of wood and glass. Luke didn't give her a chance to ask what was happening – he just grabbed her again, and rushed her down the stairs as fast as they could go.

His urgent demeanour was infectious, and he didn't need to tell her something was very wrong. She followed him as fast as she could, taking the stairs two or three at a time.

***

By the time they reached the lobby, they were out of breath and panting heavily, but he didn't let them stop. With a single smooth movement, he pushed her up against a wall and held her there while he ducked down to peer through the small glass window on the door. Even at a distance, he could see the pair of men in dark fatigues blocking the front entrance, to prevent their escape.

Luke glanced at Claudia and saw the concern etched on her features. He knew that she didn't understand – she couldn't understand – that that made his need to protect her all the more overwhelming. He snatched up her hand again, and led her down another level to the parking garage in the basement. He ignored his car, since it was well-known to the Immortelle, and ran for the exit instead.

Claudia followed him obediently as he led her across the dark space. Lights flickered on overhead as they passed, pushing back the shadows. She glanced at his car as they passed by, but she was too out of breath to ask what he was doing. Luke didn't let up though, and didn't pause to explain. He raced across the car park and up the ramp to the street beyond, startling the guard at the entrance. The security guard was a regular and Luke knew his face, so he felt no concern that he might shoot them in the back.

Perhaps I should be concerned, he thought to himself perversely, tightening his grip on Claudia's hand. It seemed like everything else in his life was made up of some kind of betrayal. There was no one that he could trust. Not even himself.

Claudia was nearing collapse from fatigue by the time he finally flagged down a taxi. He threw open the door and bundled her in, then dove in after her.

"Drive!" he gasped, startling the taxi driver with his vehemence. The cab leapt away from the curb like something out of an action movie. Luke sagged in his seat, reflecting on the fact that he hadn't gone to the gym in far too long. His body might be the picture of eternal youth, but fitness was a whole other matter.

Beside him, he heard the rasp of Claudia's breath, and the scent of her perspiration tormented him. Sometimes, the gift the elixir had bestowed upon him felt like less of a gift, and more of a curse. Today was definitely one of those days.

"Please, what's going on?" Claudia whispered. Her voice was barely audible, and he felt a soft touch on his arm. Luke glanced towards her, and felt a peculiar mix of annoyance at being asked, and pleasure at her discretion – she'd kept her voice low enough that the taxi driver wouldn't be able to make it out. It seemed she was finally beginning to appreciate the danger she was in.

It was hardly her fault, he thought as he looked down into her sweet, girlish face. He'd lied to her all along. There was no way for her to know the truth. All she'd had was a brief glimpse at his kind from the outside, which gave no real sense of depth or context. After all, it was his people that ruled the world, not hers.

In spite of his anger, Luke reached up to touch her cheek tenderly, running his thumb across the curve of her jaw before tracing it softly across her full lips. Even without cosmetics on she was lovely, exquisitely formed with cherub's bow lips and large eyes framed by long lashes.

The way she was looking at him now was so different to the way she'd looked at him when they'd first met. Gone were the scathing sideways glances and playfully mocking smiles, replaced by honest confusion, helplessness and fear. Her eyes fell closed at his touch, and he knew that she felt the hypnotic tingle of his lust even through the tips of his fingers. He regretted his gift now, and wished so desperately that he could be certain even for a moment that those looks were for him as a person, not just for his power and the pleasure that it could bring her.

"Soon," he whispered back.

When her eyes flickered open again, he shot a pointed glance towards the driver. She nodded softly, though he could see the pain that the delay caused her reflected in her eyes. It upset him to delay her when he knew she was unhappy and frightened, but his words were not for mortal ears.

He glanced away from her and stared out the window, watching the harbour roll by as their cab picked its way towards the city's edge. From within his wallet, he drew out several hundred dollar bills, and waited until the taxi stopped at traffic lights before he leaned forward to give the driver an address.

"If you get us there swiftly and without attracting any attention, then you can keep the change," he said to the driver. The man's eyes widened, then he nodded brusquely, took the money, and focused on the road.

Luke did the same, and sat back in his seat to watch where they were going with an alertness that bordered on paranoia.

The scenery changed slowly, from city to motorway and beyond. The cold concrete walls fell away to reveal sparkling blue water as they ascended, climbing the arch of the harbour bridge. Although he'd seen it a thousand times before, today it felt different — refreshing, vibrant, and so much more alive.

Luke wondered at the feeling, but before he could figure it out he was distracted by warmth against his shoulder. He glanced down and found Claudia resting her cheek against him, her eyes closed and her expression troubled. She was tired and under a great deal of stress, he realised. Sympathy blossomed within him, so he slipped his arm around her shoulders and let her nuzzle her face up against the side of his chest like a sleepy child.

Which she was, compared to him. Even as one of the youngest of the Cabal, he made most mortals look like a child by comparison. But that was her appeal, wasn't it? Everything was new to her, and watching her get excited over that newness made him regard things in a whole new light. Despite his anger at her for invading his privacy, he felt a strange sort of warmth towards her as he watched her rest. He touched her tenderly and ran his fingertips through her hair, feeling an unexpected affection towards the girl that had interrupted the monotony of his life.

She was supposed to be his mate. He knew his father's plans for them, even though he wasn't supposed to. Like her, inquisitiveness was in his nature, so he couldn't be too angry with her for what she'd done. The desire to know was a powerful instinct, especially when it concerned one's own fate.

His father had planned for her to join them, to take the elixir and become one of the Immortelle, and then for Luke to impregnate her. The genetic blending was forecast to produce great gifts in their offspring, a greater affinity for the Power than ever seen before.

What his father hadn't planned on was Luke developing feelings for her.

He really should have known better. While William's blood ran ice cold after so many years of immortality, Luke was still young and hot-blooded. Luke knew that he, himself, had been selectively bred to advance the Cabal's plans, just as Claudia had been – just as the Cabal had planned for his future offspring to be. A few weeks ago, he'd regarded the plan with little interest, just a pleasant diversion from the sameness of his years.

Now, as he looked at her, he felt a great sense of rage curdle in his gut. He'd used her. His father had used her. Her own mother had used her. She was an innocent pawn in the whole game, and for the first time in a very long time Luke felt terrible anger over his role in the Cabal's affairs.

She was asleep now, he realised suddenly. Her face had relaxed at last, and through their physical connection he could feel the faintest reflection of her dreams. He frowned, confused – it usually took years for members of his Cabal to develop that kind of connection with someone. Curious, he closed his eyes and focused on her mind.

In her dream, he saw a man, handsome, naked, and gentle. Luke felt a stab of jealousy, until he realised that the man he saw was himself, reflected through her eyes. It was an intimate dream, intense and sexual – his presence affected her just as strongly as hers affected him.

Probably even more so, he thought with a twinge of

guilt. His body oozed sex when he was even the slightest bit aroused, an unfortunate side-effect of his link to the Power. His pheromones affected the people around him in the most base, animal way. Claudia was no exception.

Unfortunately, his attraction to her meant that when she became aroused, he did as well. In response, his pheromones grew stronger, and they excited her more. As her lust mounted, her scent tormented him and made his own feelings more and more intense. It was a vicious cycle that could only end in one way.

He closed his eyes and grimaced, trying in vain not to think about her. About the feel of her slender body beneath his arm, the scent of her hair, the touch of her skin... it was so difficult, and yet for her sake he tried.

Eventually and with great discomfort, his heart-rate slowed and gradually returned to normal. He drew slow, deep breaths through his mouth, forcing himself to relax and ignore the scent of her all around him. It was painfully difficult, but at last he succeeded in wrangling his out-of-control hormones into some semblance of order. His reward was watching Claudia's dreams grow less intense.

Once the overwhelming animal lust between them finally faded, he stroked her hair thoughtfully and let her dreams dance through his mind. Her sleeping mind responded to the change, but to his surprise he still featured heavily in her subconscious. Now, he felt her dreaming of the moments they'd spent together in quiet time at work, talking and laughing, and he felt the burden of conscience that weighed heavily upon her. Even in peaceful sleep, he felt her remorse for what she'd done to him.

Remorse, from her? That both surprised and pleased

him. If the emotional consequences of her actions bothered her, then some part of her must care about his feelings. In a strange sort of way, that gave him hope that they might really have some kind of future together.

If, of course, they managed to survive the day.

Chapter Seven

It had been a long day, and Claudia was exhausted. At first her sleep was troubled, plagued by lurid memories of her early morning tryst with the handsome immortal. Eventually, the blind heat of passion faded away and left her feeling drained. Her dreams became sad and wistful in a strange, upsetting way.

Even unconscious, she felt regret over violating Luke's privacy. She'd done it to others before and in far worse ways – prying was her job. And yet this time, she felt like she'd broken some cardinal law, and shattered a fragile bond of trust that she hadn't even realised was developing between them until she'd carelessly destroyed it.

She vaguely heard when the taxi came to a halt through her comfortable half-doze. With great effort, she dragged herself back out of that warm place and grudgingly opened her eyes. The sun was brighter than she expected and made her blink owlishly. Somehow, it had become mid-afternoon while she'd napped, and they'd left the city far behind them.

Luke slipped the taxi driver another small bundle of notes to guarantee his silence, and then he looked at her.

"You might want to put your shoes on," he said, his voice soft and gentle. She looked past him out the window, and saw rolling green meadows spanning out in all directions. There was no trace of civilization to be seen, not even farmhouses or sign posts. The road they were on was barely more than a dirt track. It was not terrain for high heels, so Claudia opened her purse and pulled a pair of small, rolled-up flats out of her emergency kit, kept there just in case of circumstances like this.

Well, not exactly like this, she thought to herself. There was no way she could have anticipated this happening. Her feet still hurt from their madcap dash from the apartment, but she refused to complain about it. Even with no explanation forthcoming, she sensed that Luke had saved her life.

The immortal's vivid blue eyes watched her with interest as she unrolled the little shoes and put them on. The intensity of his expression made her feel strange, simultaneously flattered and embarrassed.

"Mother taught me to be prepared," she said, tilting her head towards her heels. "Stilettos aren't exactly the most versatile footwear. Sometimes you need an alternative in a hurry. As much as I adore my Jimmy Choos, four inch heels in overgrown, grassy paddocks is just asking for trouble."

"Practical, and accurate," Luke said, nodding his approval, then he opened the door and climbed out. He turned back towards her and surprised her with a gentlemanly offer of a hand to assist her. She took it without thinking, and let him help her to her feet. His hand brushed against the small of her back as he leaned past her to fetch her purse and heels from the back seat, and then he closed the taxi's door. She took her purse from him and put it over her shoulder, then together they watched as the taxi rolled away.

By the time it had vanished into the distance, Luke was already walking, though she had no idea how he knew where he was going. Every direction looked the same to her. Survival training was not something her mother had considered remotely useful to her, so it hadn't been included in her education. She hurried to catch up with him and fell into step at his side.

It was warm in the midsummer sun, but a light breeze kept her cool as they walked across the fields towards a distant line of hills. All around her, long grass rippled like flowing silk in the wind. The air smelt fresh and clean, nothing like her home in Australia, where it was always hot and the wind carried the permanent scent of either the desert, the ocean, or some peculiar hybrid of both.

Claudia shot a glance towards her companion, and found him staring off into the middle distance as though he could see something that she could not. Which she considered was entirely possible, given that he'd already shown an assortment of preternatural abilities. Guessing the limits of his powers was futile, because she didn't have any grounds for comparison.

She reached out to touch his fingertips with her own, wondering whether he'd forgiven her for snooping or whether he was leading her to her doom. As though sensing her thoughts, he slipped his hand around hers and held it softly, reassuringly, letting her draw comfort from his strength.

There were so many questions that she longed to ask, and yet she knew he would only answer them when he was ready.

She didn't even know how old he was. In silence, she stared down at the grass and pondered the question as they walked. Had he lived through the great world wars? Survived the fall of the Roman Empire? Had he observed from on high as the great pyramids were built? The texts she'd found suggested that all that and more was entirely possible, but again she had no grounds for comparison.

He had said that he was one of the youngest, but what did that even mean?

"I turned ninety-eight last November," Luke said suddenly, which startled her since she hadn't asked the question out loud. She stared at him, wide-eyed, while he continued to speak in soft, even tones.

***

"I was born on the eve of what's come to be referred to as the First World War," he told her. "It was shortly after the second that I received the gift. My clan originates from southern Europe, but many of us found the behaviour of our eastern European brethren at that time to be distasteful, and left the area long before it reached the point of open conflict. I had no idea at that stage, though – I was still mortal, and ignorant of the Cabal's existence. My father sent me to Britain before the war broke out, to study at Cambridge University. Despite my Italian citizenship, they let me enlist and fight with the Allies. They needed every warm body they could get."

"Wait – you mentioned your eastern European brethren," Claudia interrupted. "Do you mean Adolf Hitler was one of your kind?"

"No, though I hear he aspired to it." Luke grimaced, as though the thought was repulsive to him. "The man who at the time called himself Himmler is, though. If I remember correctly, he's your mother's great-uncle. Or was it a cousin? Matters of relationship get complicated when generations can span several millennia."

"You're using the present tense," Claudia pointed out. "Every school child knows that Heinrich Himmler committed suicide at the end of the Second World War."

"Yes, and Nicholas Romanov was *really* executed." Luke stopped walking suddenly and turned to her. "Claudia, when I told you that nothing is true and everything is permitted, I was not merely quoting Bartol. Nothing in this world is as you know it. The man history knows as Nicholas Romanov, the last Tsar of Russia, gave himself a new face and rules again beneath the name Putin. John F. Kennedy now lives a quiet life in England, waiting for the generations to pass so his face is forgotten. A staged assassination or a closed-door execution is one of the preferred ways for our more prominent members to withdraw from society without having anyone notice that they never grow old."

Claudia stared at him, obviously stunned beyond words. A faint smile twitched Luke's lips as he reached up and gently took her by the shoulders. "My own father, the man you know as William Logan, once practiced law in the city-state of Athens under the name of Solon. You may have heard of him."

Her mouth fell open and she stared him, unable to process so much information all at once. Luke felt a surge of amusement at the look on her face, but sympathy as well. It hadn't been all that long ago that his father had given him the same talk, and he still remembered how it felt. Suddenly, he realised that there were tears in her eyes, and he worried that perhaps he'd been too blunt.

Again, she surprised him.

"I always suspected that 'Lucio Cavenelli' wasn't your real name," she said. She sniffed hard to restrain the tears and tilted her head back a bit, staring up at the lovely blue sky above them.

Luke laughed and shook his head. "No, I was born with a different family name. I've kept my given name so far, though. Usually, we take a whole new name when we change identities, since it gets a little obvious if you keep names that are too similar. I've heard that some of the Slavs like to keep their names and make excuses to cover the similarities, but the rest of us are more subtle than that. But you don't critique the Slavs. They're... enigmatic."

Claudia managed a weak smile, but he could tell she was overwhelmed. He understood. He'd just ripped the carpet out from beneath her whole understanding of the world, and he wasn't done yet.

"What about my family?" she asked softly. "You mentioned my mother. Do you know who my father is?"

"Soon, Claudia. Very soon." Luke wrapped his arms around her slender frame and drew her up against his chest. "Sadly, we have no more time to talk right now. Brace yourself."

A moment later, the ground collapsed beneath them and they tumbled into darkness.

***

Claudia awoke to the sound of dripping water. She felt the warmth of arms wrapped around her, but also the chill of stone beneath her legs. Although she felt discomfort when she moved, it was a dull ache rather than searing pain so she judged herself to be more or less uninjured.

When her eyes opened, she found herself in a deep hole illuminated by sunlight streaming in through the orifice above her head. Luke knelt at her side, cradling her in his arms, but his face was hard and tense as he stared around.

"W-what happened?" she whispered, carefully easing

herself up into a sitting position. Her head spun, but she tested her limbs and found each one undamaged. A glance around told her an even more peculiar truth: the hole they were in seemed to have formed spontaneously beneath them. The floor was even and regular and made of solid stone, but the walls and ceiling were simply earth. It was too perfect, too tidy. Unnatural, somehow. She didn't know how, but they'd been trapped deliberately, like a pair of rabbits in a pitfall.

"They noticed we're here." Luke's voice was tense and irritable, but she sensed his annoyance wasn't directed at her. "And now they're making us wait at their leisure." Suddenly, he seemed to remember she was there and shot a look of concern at her. "Are you injured?"

"No," she said, shaking her head. "Just confused. Where are we, why, and who are 'they'?"

A smile graced his lips, and she felt the touch of his hand delicately tracing her jaw. He was about to say something when they were interrupted by a heavily-accented voice from above.

"Now that is excellent question. Why *are* you here, incubus?"

They looked up together. Silhouetted against the afternoon sun, a male figure stood watching them, perched impossibly close to the lip of the hole. Luke stood and helped her up, then shot a glare at the figure above them. "Is this how you greet guests now, Piotr? Your hospitality isn't as good as I remember it."

"Last time you entered our territory, our clans were still allies. A lot has changed since then, has it not?" The voice was ripe with sarcasm. Claudia recognised the accent as eastern European, the kind of accent that devoured his syllables whole, turned 'that' into 'zat', and bit his w's clean in half. "And what is this, a mortal?

You realise that you've signed her death warrant now."

"I don't think so," Luke replied, his voice low and dangerous. He glanced at Claudia for just a moment, but the words he spoke struck her like a blow to the face. "In fact, I think your high elder would kill you if you harmed her. This is Claudia. His daughter."

Chapter Eight

Claudia stumbled. The rope binding her hands behind her back made it hard for her to balance, but her guard caught her and jerked her upright before she could fall. She bit her lip to fight back a cry as the rope dug cruelly into her wrists, and blinked back the tears that threatened to mar her vision.

The experience of being a prisoner was not one that she cared to repeat, but at least she was better off than Luke. She was only bound by a nylon cord around her wrists. He was in chains and could barely move, let alone walk. She shot a worried glance at him, and was rewarded by a shove from one of the men guarding her.

Again, she stumbled. Again, she was caught — but this time, she was sworn at as well. Try as she might to keep her emotions under lock and key, a tear escaped and rolled down her cheek. Nothing in her twenty-six years of life could have prepared her for this.

After the revelation of her paternity, they'd been rescued from their hole, restrained, stripped of their belongings, and forced to walk for what felt like forever across flat green pasturelands. The only problem was, this was no longer a stroll in the country — now, it was a forced march. Her flimsy shoes were hardly fit for the task, and the ground around her was uneven. While the men around her were sure-footed and confident in their heavy boots, she was not.

Her foot struck the edge of an indentation hidden beneath the grass, and she fell heavily to her knees.

***

Luke watched as Claudia struggled back to her feet before her captors could grab her, and marched on proudly with her chin held high, but he saw the gleam of her tears in her eyes. Raw fury surged through him, threatening his control.

He rounded on the man called Piotr, and the Power flared up around him like a violent, invisible storm. Even with his hands and feet chained, he was not helpless. He locked eyes with his enemy and that was enough: Piotr was frozen, caught in the cobra's gaze.

"I am your enemy, not her," Luke hissed through clenched teeth. "So, if your men must abuse someone, then let it be me, and leave her alone. Or have you forgotten how to treat ladies with respect?"

Luke heard Claudia cry a warning, but he didn't duck in time; the butt of a gun struck him hard on the back of the head. The Power faded as he crumpled to the ground, and released Piotr from its grasp.

***

"Don't hurt him!" Claudia cried. Panic surged through her, and she lashed out at the man restraining her with all of her strength, planting a solid kick on his shin. It did no real damage, but it hurt enough to surprise him. His grip loosened for a second, just long enough for her to twist away. She rushed to Luke's side and threw herself to her knees beside him, shielding him with her body. The man who had hit Luke cursed bitterly at her and raised his weapon again, intending to strike her as well.

She squeezed her eyes closed so that she wouldn't see the blow coming, as if ignorance would somehow make it hurt less. Although she was skilled in many ways, Claudia had little experience with physical pain, and she was terrified of it.

But, the blow never came.

When she finally worked up the courage to open her eyes, she found the stranger, Piotr, holding back the gun that would have struck her. He watched her with a troubled expression on his face, as if he couldn't quite figure out what she was doing.

"Enough," the big man rumbled. He gave his guardsman a sharp look, then released his grip and turned to her. Without another word, he knelt and picked her up as easily as a child, tossing her over his shoulder in a fireman's carry. Her first thought was to protest, but that was quickly replaced by common sense. Even the indignity of being carried like that was better than falling on her face every few paces. Her concern was for Luke.

With great difficulty, she managed to lift her head enough to look back at him, and saw him being picked up and carried by two other men. Reassured that he wasn't being harmed, she flopped back down against the man's broad back and tried to relax.

The trip went much faster without them tripping in their bonds. Within minutes, they crossed the threshold of the house, but Claudia was too dizzy to take much notice. All the blood had rushed to her head, and she hung limp with her eyes closed trying to fight down nausea. For the first time all day, she was glad she hadn't eaten anything since mid-afternoon the day before, since that meant there was nothing in her to come back up.

The voices of the men fanned off in different directions, and she heard rather than saw her captor climbing stairs. A door creaked as it was opened, then she felt herself being shifted. After a moment of disorientation, gravity returned to its proper place, and she opened her eyes to find herself sitting on the edge of a bed.

Piotr stood over her, absently scratching his chin as he considered her with a cryptic eye. He was large and muscular, with close-cropped blond hair and steel-grey eyes – handsome, in a way, but Claudia was too miserable to notice. She was more concerned about the fact that Luke was no longer in sight, and she was alone with an intimidatingly large man.

All her brash self-confidence was gone, crushed by the fact that she was surrounded by people that could squash her with a thought. She gave in to misery for a moment, and hung her head, staring at the floor. What had Luke been thinking?

"Hmph." Piotr made an indignant sound, his expression turning derisive. "You cannot be the daughter of our leader. Look at you cowering from me, bah. No wonder the incubus has you wrapped around his little finger."

A flash of rage blasted away her self-pity. Claudia's head jerked up, and she fixed the big man with a glare.

"Hey, fuck you, mate," she growled, her carefully-hidden Australian accent emerging in a rare moment of carelessness. "I've had a hell of a bad day. I've been knocked unconscious twice, chased barefoot across half the city, and I'm surrounded by immortal bastards who are looking for any reason to kill me just because I don't have any way to fight back. It's a bloody rough day in Mortal Town, so why don't you just go fuck yourself? Oh, and for the record, he's the one wrapped around *my* little finger – not the other way around!"

Piotr's brows rose over the course of her tirade, and he stood back watching her with his arms folded across his barrel chest. When she finally paused for breath, he chuckled and shook his head.

"Ah, so you do have fire in you, little one. Interesting." He paused to consider for a moment, and then moved around behind her to free her hands. "I will untie you. Do not try anything foolish. As you said, you have no chance against us. We will fetch you once we have contacted the man you claim is your father."

"That *Luke* claims is my father," she said, glaring at him. "I don't know anything about that. I only know who my mother is." When the last knot came undone and her hands were freed, Claudia rubbed her wrists and heaved a sigh of relief. Then a twinge of concern struck her, and she turned to look at the large blond man. "What about Luke?"

"Luke is our blood enemy, and will be treated as such," Piotr said, dismissing the question with a gesture, then he walked past her towards the door.

"Wait!" Claudia leapt to her feet and reached out to touch his arm, restraining him for a moment. He glanced back at her, only to find her staring up at him plaintively, the fire in her eyes replaced by genuine concern. "Please don't hurt him. He saved my life, and he brought me here knowing full well that you might likely kill him. He did it selflessly, to try and protect me. I-I care about him... please, if you have any trace of humanity left in your soul, don't hurt him."

Staring up into the man's hard, angular face, Claudia felt hopelessness flood through her all over again. At first it seemed that her heart-felt appeal had no effect, but when her eyes dropped away to hide the emotion welling up in them, his expression softened just the tiniest bit.

"I will see what I can do," he said, then he walked out of the room, leaving her all alone. She heard a key rattle in the lock, and knew that she was trapped. With nothing else to do but wait, she flopped back down on the bed she'd been given and wrestled against the dark emotions that threatened to overwhelm her.

***

She managed to get a couple of hours sleep, curled up fully dressed atop the blankets, but her sleep was troubled, tormented by images of her lover in pain. When she awoke, the sun had set and plunged the room into darkness. Fumbling around in the dark, she managed to find a light switch to illuminate her gilded cage.

The bedroom appeared to be part of a suite, furnished in the old country style. Roses adorned the bedspread and the curtains, and portraits of fruit hung on the walls. Somehow, it managed to be both personal and impersonal at the same time, like a cut-out from a magazine on interior design, or a photo from a hotel's brochure.

There was a small bathroom attached, but it was nothing more than a toilet and a sink. Lacking any other option, she retreated there for a while to relieve herself and wash off the mud and grass stains as best she could. With the aid of a small hand towel, she managed a fairly decent job of making herself look presentable, but her hair was a mess, her clothing was rumpled, and she had no access to the tools she needed to make herself look any better.

With no other choice but to try her luck, she wandered over to the door and tapped on it softly.

There was a gruff reply from the other side in a language she recognised as Scandinavian, but did not understand.

"Is there any chance I could get my purse, please?" she called back, but the response she got was short and curt, followed by harsh laughter, which she presumed meant the answer was no.

With a heavy sigh, she returned to her bed and curled up again, to pass the hours of her imprisonment in sleep.

***

She jerked awake again in the middle of the night, her slumber interrupted by the sound of heavy boots on the stairs outside her room. She sat up and stared expectantly at the door; sure enough, a few seconds later a key rattled in the lock, and then Piotr opened the door.

When he saw she was awake, he beckoned for her to follow him. She considered her options briefly, but none of them seemed terribly appealing so she just rose and did as she was told. There was no point in wasting energy putting up a fight if she had no real way of escaping – and besides, she couldn't abandon Luke. The idea of leaving him behind felt criminally wrong, after everything he'd done to try and save her life.

As she padded barefoot down the stairs, she drew strength from her training to mask her own concerns. She threw back her shoulders and straightened her back, putting as much dignity into her poise as she could. Piotr led her into the room that had once served as the living room for the little country manor. To her surprise, she discovered it had been stripped bare and replaced by a mind-boggling array of technological devices. Along the wall to her left, an enormous television had been converted into a video conference monitor. On it, a stern face watched her enter with intensely-vivid turquoise eyes.

Much like Piotr and many of the other men, the man on the monitor was blond and handsome in an angular sort of way, but the difference was that this man positively oozed power. Without taking any cues from her captors, Claudia stepped forward to stand directly in front of the monitor, staring intently at the image on the screen.

There was definitely a physical resemblance, she thought as she examined him. Her hair was more white-blonde like her mother's than ash blond like his, but they shared the same unusual turquoise eyes. His expression was cold and implacable, so she made a snap decision: coyness would get her nowhere with a person like that. This time, she sensed that boldness would get her what she wanted.

"Are you my father?" she asked the question suddenly. There was a faint twitch of a brow and she saw his jaw tighten, but that was the only sign of emotion on the man's hard, angular face.

"I know nothing of any daughter," he snapped in a voice that was thick with a German accent. "It is your claim that you are my child, is it not?"

"No. I have no idea who my father is, I've never met him," she answered just as bluntly. "I only know who my mother is. The first I heard about any of this was when Luke brought me here."

"Who is your mother?" the man demanded, his expression as cold and impassive as a glacier.

"Antoinette Bell," she replied. "At least, that's the name I know her by. I don't know if it's her real name."

There was another twitch of a brow. Claudia knew immediately that he recognised the name. To any other, the tiny elements of his body language might have gone unnoticed, but in her moment of greatest need she found her skills still coming in useful.

"You know her, don't you?" Claudia asked softly. It was neither an accusation nor a question – it was a statement. His faint grimace told her all that she needed to know.

"There was a moment of indiscretion some years ago," he admitted, and stared at her with greater interest now. "But I do not understand how this could happen. We have greater control over such things than you mortals. I did not choose to impregnate her."

"I don't know anything about that. It was before I was born," Claudia said dryly, though there was no true humour in her tone. "I suspect Luke knows more, though. Perhaps you should ask him."

The man on the monitor glanced past her, to where Piotr stood impassive by the door. She looked over her shoulder as well, and watched as he nodded curtly and left the room. With the conversation suspended, silence descended on the room.

A few minutes later, she heard Piotr coming back. The sound of chains rattling against wood reached them long before the door opened, and Piotr led in a heavily-manacled Luke. Claudia was relieved to see he only had a few more bruises than when she'd last seen him, but she still felt her stomach lurch at the sight of him in irons.

His hands were cuffed behind his back, and a thick chain ran between his wrists and the steel collar locked about his throat. Piotr led him to her side, and then forced him to his knees beside her with one huge hand on his shoulder. Although he knelt without complaint, Luke's expression was tense and alert. He was obedient, but not submissive.

Despite the danger of the situation, Claudia knelt beside him. He gave her a long-suffering smile when she touched his cheek in concern, then he startled her by asking about her health in spite of his own condition. "Are you all right, Claudia?"

"I was about to ask you the same thing." She shot an appealing look over her shoulder at the monitor. "Is this really necessary? He came here willingly."

"It is necessary until I decide otherwise," the man on the monitor said. Claudia opened her mouth to protest, but she was silenced by Luke.

"Hush, Claudia. It's all right," he said gently. He gave her a reassuring smile, and then turned his attention to the stern man on the monitor. "Herr Gunther, forgive me for interrupting your schedule, and thank you for your hospitality. I present to you your daughter, Claudia, conceived through a terrible betrayal committed by Antoinette Bell twenty-seven years ago. I hope that you can forgive Claudia for the sins of her mother, as she is innocent of that crime."

"Betrayal?" Claudia echoed, bewildered. "You never said anything about my mother being a traitor."

Luke looked at her, his face marred by sadness. "I suggest that you sit down. As loathe as I am to hurt you, you are not going to like the truth."

***

Silence descended as Luke told the tale of Antoinette's betrayal. He explained how, many years before, her loyalty had been seduced away from her own clan by the wiles of the Cabal.

In brief sentences, he explained for Claudia's sake that the Immortelle were divided into clans by the approximate geographic area in which they had evolved. The Cabal, the group to which Luke and William Logan belonged, had its base of power in Italy, France and Spain. The name had been given to them mockingly by the other clans for their diabolical, manipulative ways, but they had claimed it for their own and now spoke it with pride.

Antoinette, on the other hand, was from the clan that ruled Germany, Denmark, Sweden, and the Netherlands, as well as many other parts of Western Europe. They called themselves the Führung, 'the Leaders' in German, and Claudia and Luke were currently in one of their safe houses.

"I am not certain how far back Antoinette's betrayal goes," Luke admitted, his expression neutral. "I know she was our creature long before the plot to conceive Claudia was born. I also know that when Antoinette seduced you, several of our strongest clan members were on hand nearby. They manipulated your mind, High Elder. They used the Power to warp your thoughts so that you chose to impregnate her, and then afterwards they concealed your memory of the event."

The man on the screen twitched around the edges and Claudia could see cold fury building in his eyes. "Why?"

"They wanted to mate her to me," Luke said simply.

"Excuse me?" Claudia exclaimed, staring at her lover in shock. Of all the answers she had expected, that was not it. Anger started to bubble up in her chest, but before it could explode, Luke shot her a look that told her exactly how he felt about that plan – and about her.

"I am sorry, Claudia," he said softly to her, as if they were alone in the room. "I only found out about this a few months ago, myself. My clan has experimented with selective breeding for generations, seeking to create a more powerful immortal." His gaze lowered and he drew a deep breath, to steady himself. "I've always known that I was selectively bred. Most of the younger members of my clan are, unless someone decides to add new blood to the mix. Even then, it's usually carefully planned."

"And that's what I was supposed to be?" she asked, bewildered and horrified by the concept. "New blood for your Cabal's breeding pool?"

Luke shook his head. "No, if you became one of the Immortelle, you would still have the abilities of a member of the Führung clan, even if your loyalties were owned by the Cabal. But, our offspring would have the genetic potential to merge the strengths of the Cabal and Führung bloodlines, and become more adept with the Power than either of us."

"What makes you think I would even want to have a child with you?" Claudia snapped, the rage surging through her all over again. Luke's head jerked up again and the look he gave her was one of such hurt that she immediately regretted her words.

"It wasn't my idea," he said, pain echoing in his vibrant blue eyes. "When I found out, I asked the same question. I was told that I was expected to manipulate your mind into accepting my seed, the same way we manipulated your father. Please, my love – don't be angry with me."

His voice pleaded with her, but she couldn't figure out how to feel. She looked away, hid her face behind her hand, and drew slow, deep breaths to try and contain her anger. She had been conceived for no better reason than to be used as a vessel for some powerful child? All her life, all her training, her mother's coaching and her schooling, for what? To have a convenient excuse for her to be hired at Cornelius Pharmaceuticals, so that she could be seduced and impregnated?

"You said you didn't know who my father was," she said softly, but the softness was a mask of deception to hide her fury. "You lied to me. And when you told me that you had been ordered to seduce me in order to assess me, was any of that true, or were you just lying to me again?" She knew that she was being watched closely by the immortals all around her, but she just didn't care.

"Yes. I swear to you, I have never done or said anything to deliberately hurt or undermine you," he answered, his eyes appealing even though he couldn't move. Unable to look at him any longer, she turned away, shaking her head.

"How am I supposed to believe that?" she said bitterly. "You're just as bad as the rest of them, all of you are. Truth and perceived truth, lies and selective breeding – I want nothing to do with any of this." Feeling terribly betrayed, she turned sharply on her heel and stormed off towards the door. Piotr stood aside as she approached and let her out into the hall.

There was no reason for them to worry, after all. She had no idea where she was and couldn't leave anyway. Her only choice was to retreat back to the relative sanctuary of the room upstairs, where she could be alone with her thoughts for a while.

Although she heard Luke call her name as she left, she couldn't bear to look at him just yet. The plaintive appeal in his voice made her cringe internally, but she didn't show it. With straight-backed pride, she marched herself right back up the stairs and sequestered herself in her room.

Then the moment that she was alone, emotion came bubbling out and she found herself in tears. It was too much for her to bear all at once, and she was exhausted and hungry as well. With the tears streaming unrestrained down her cheeks, she retreated to the tiny bathroom and stuck her face beneath the tap, to drink deeply of the cool, clean water in order to relieve her thirst. Once she was quenched, she flopped down on the cold tiles and wrapped her arms around her legs.

How could I have been so stupid? She buried her face in her knees, silently cursing herself. Layer upon layer of deception wrapped itself around these people, and not a single thing that she thought she knew could be confirmed as true. She'd seen right through Luke's deception from the start, and yet she'd still let herself fall for him.

If everything she knew was a lie, then how could she possibly trust anyone?

Chapter Nine

Hours later, Claudia heard her door open. Heavily-booted footsteps thundered across the floor, but she was still trapped in a cycle of anger and denial, and didn't really care. Piotr's shadow fell across her when he stepped into the bathroom, but she was too enraged to even notice him at first.

"Up." The big man's voice was gentle, and so were his hands. He picked her up as easily as if she were a toddler, and set her on her feet. "I have brought you food. Eat."

Claudia just glared at him wordlessly until he left alone, but the smell of hot food did bring her back to her senses. She padded out into the bedroom, where she found a tray waiting for her with a bowl of meat and vegetable stew, and a few slices of thick, black bread slathered with butter.

Her stomach growled, reminding her it had been more than a day since she'd last eaten. By the time she sat down, her mouth was watering and her stomach was twisting itself into knots. Despite that, she ate slowly to avoid making herself sick. She knew that she would need every ounce of strength in the coming days.

As she ate, her blind fury began to ebb and her thoughts became less hostile. She discovered a kind of clarity in the monotonous chore of eating that brooding had denied her. At last, she was able to think about the last few months without going back into an uncontrollable rage.

Luke was at the top of her thoughts, unsurprisingly. His kindness and generosity bewildered her. Those looks that he had given her, and the way he'd called her his love – it made no sense to her. How could he love her when he barely knew her? She could only guess that life worked differently for immortals. He'd seen four generations rise and fall, and yet he was still considered to be a child by the standards of his people. Perhaps he really did love her, or at least thought that he loved her, which was close enough. He'd given up everything to protect her.

Right now, he was probably in chains somewhere, suffering because of her. If he'd just done what his clan had told him, then they would probably still be in bed in his apartment, lost in a world of overwhelming passion that would end with her bearing a child she wasn't ready for and didn't really want.

Claudia sighed softly. The thought of him trapped and alone because of her made her feel ill. She had no desire to cause him any pain, not after what he'd been through to protect her. Now that she'd absorbed the truth and recovered from the shock, she desperately wanted to see him again, to be sure he was all right and to ask him all those burning questions that she couldn't ask in public.

As she finished the last of her food, she thought over her options and decided on the bold course of action again. It had worked well last time, so perhaps it would work again. The people she was with, the Führung, they seemed to respect boldness. She wondered if that was why her mother had raised her that way.

Claudia rose quickly and straightened up her

clothing, tucking her crumpled blouse into the waist of her skirt. With her fingers, she combed her hair as best she could, though she longed for a brush to get the tangles out properly. No time for that now, though. Perhaps later.

She threw back her shoulders and put on her best expression of total confidence, then strode over to the door and tried the handle. It was unlocked. When she opened it, she discovered a single guard seated outside. He was lazing in a chair with his gun across his lap, paying more attention to his mobile phone than to guarding her.

He glanced up in surprise when the door opened, and she caught his eye with a look of intense scrutiny.

"Take me to Luke," she said. "Now."

It wasn't a request, it was an order. The man hesitated for only a moment, then he nodded, stood up, and led her back down the stairs. She swallowed a surge of pride and followed after him. At the base of the stairs, the man opened a door and led her down another staircase into darkness, then she found herself in a network of corridors beneath the house. It was cold, and the air tasted damp and earthy, but the walls were reassuringly solid stone. Another guard loitered nearby, who was very nearly a carbon copy of the one she was following. They were both huge and silent, but obedient.

The second guard just looked at her. This time, she didn't have to say a thing. He knew what she wanted, and hastened to obey. She didn't know whether they were responding to her demeanour or her possible relationship with their leader, and she didn't care so long as they did as they were told.

The first guard returned to his post as the second one took over the task of leading her deep into the warren of cold stone passages. There were doors set into the walls, but as she passed them she realised none of the doors had hinges, locks, or even door handles. Like the walls, they were solid stone. She wondered how they opened.

She didn't have to wonder for long. The guard stopped in front of one of the strange doors and gestured for her to stand back. She did so, curious to see what he was going to do.

The guardsman reached out and placed his palm against the stone slab, with an expression of intense concentration. Claudia felt something strange in the air, like the crackling of static electricity before a storm – then suddenly the stone split and crumbled as though made of nothing more than sand. It dissolved away until she could see the room beyond, a low, dark cell lit only by the murky glow of an ancient light bulb on the ceiling.

She stepped through and spotted Luke slumped against the far wall. He was bound to the stone, his wrists suspended on chains too short for him to be able to either stand or lie down with any degree of comfort. Claudia felt a twinge of sympathy when she noticed he'd gained a few more bruises since the last time she'd seen him, and she wondered if they were her fault.

His head came up at the sound of her footsteps. As their eyes met, she saw the confusing mix of emotions that he was wrestling with, as well as the physical discomfort he was in. They'd taken his jacket away, and left him dressed in just his pants and a rumpled dress shirt that hung open in the front. The heavy steel collar was still around his throat, and she could see at a glance that he was having trouble lifting his head because of its weight.

A soft hissing sound startled her. She glanced back over her shoulder, and saw the door reforming at the guard's will. Within moments, the sand had swirled up to fill the entire space, then it seemed to melt and liquefy, leaving behind a solid wall of stone.

"That's quite a trick," she said.

"The members of the Führung possess the ability to manipulate the natural world to various degrees," Luke explained, his voice hoarse from captivity and thirst. She glanced around and saw a large bottle of water sitting nearby, but realised with great annoyance that it had been deliberately placed just beyond his reach.

"And your people – your Cabal – they possess the ability to control minds?" she asked. She fetched the bottle as she spoke, and his eyes followed her all the way, but he didn't ask for it, didn't beg for her help. He seemed to be resigned to his fate, because it was a fate that he had chosen to spare her from pain.

"Amongst other things," he admitted, dropping his gaze.

Her gut twisted at the sight of him beaten and chained. She knelt in front of him, and opened the water bottle. His gaze flicked back up again, watching her, but still he didn't beg – and Claudia had no intention of making him do so. She understood the discomfort of thirst, so she didn't make him wait or try to manipulate answers from him in exchange for water. That would have been too cruel, and she couldn't bear to watch any creature suffer like that, especially not someone that she liked. Instead, she held the water up to his lips and helped him to drink as much as he could handle safely. His eyes closed in obviously relief as the water rolled down his parched throat, and she felt terribly guilty for being responsible for making him feel that way. She didn't know if immortals could die from hunger or thirst, but she could see it was still unpleasant for him.

When he was sated, his head sagged again, pulled down by the weight of the collar around his neck. She reached up and brushed a droplet of water from his lips, her own discomfort feeling so minor compared to what he was going through. Still, she needed answers - that was why she'd come.

"What kind of 'other things'?" she asked gently, trailing her fingers along his cheek.

"Mostly sexual things," he replied. His voice was just as soft, and he grimaced as though it brought him shame to admit it. "We are different, biologically, and not just for being immortal. Once we drink of the Elixir of Life, we… mutate, for lack of a better word. Those of the Cabal bloodlines become creatures that thrive off sex."

"So that's why Piotr called you an incubus?" she asked. He nodded, but the revelation only made him look more miserable.

"Yes." He hung his head, looking truly ashamed. "When we are aroused even the slightest, our bodies ooze pheromones that make us irresistible to the opposite sex. Some of the older brethren can control it, but I am too young. I managed to, once, for your sake – in the taxi on the way out here."

"While I was napping?" she asked. "I wondered what happened there, my dreams were very strange. Why did you bother?"

"I—" He paused, looking uncomfortable, but after a moment of indecision he admitted the truth. "Sexual attraction is both our weakness as well as our strength. The reason my father insisted that I seduce you was because in the moment of orgasm, you would share your thoughts and memories with me. For a moment, I knew everything there was to know about you. I could learn if you intended us harm or if you were a double-agent."

Claudia sat quietly while he spoke, sensing that he needed to tell her the truth – the whole truth, with no embellishments and no apologies. This was his chance to tell her everything and to find out if she really could understand him. In a strange way, she thought that might be possible.

"But occasionally, we also develop a bond with the target of our desires," Luke admitted. He lifted his head and looked at her, his eyes sad and appealing. "Sometimes, when you touch me I can hear what you're thinking or feel your emotions. When you were resting against me, I saw your dreams and realised that my pheromones were making you distressed. I don't want to hurt you. Ever."

This time, it was Claudia who broke eye contact first; the thought of someone reading her mind all the time was not a pleasant one. "Is that the only reason you did all this - because you don't want to hurt me?"

"No." She heard his chains rattle as he shifted around trying to touch her, but he couldn't quite reach her. "I think... I think I'm in love with you, Claudia. This collar they have me in, it's made of a special metal called cold iron. Cold iron is one of the most valuable metals on the planet, because it is the only thing that can suppress the powers of an Immortelle. Right now, I'm almost as mortal as you are. But even without my body craving you mindlessly and begging me to touch you, you're all that I can think about. The only conclusion I can come to is that this is what love feels like."

"You're human right now?" she echoed. "So there are no lust-inducing pheromones? No mental manipulation? Just you and me, as human beings?"

"Well, I'm still immortal, but yes." Their eyes met and he gave her the faintest of smiles. "At the moment,

I am just a regular man. You see me now as I was in the early 1940s. Just a man."

She rolled the thought over in her head as she stared at him, considering the possibilities. It was strangely fascinating. Just like that, the immortal that had held so much power over her before had been reduced to someone no more powerful than she was. The more she thought about it, the more she liked the idea.

Before she quite realised what she was doing, she found herself reaching for him, running the tips of her fingers across his firm, muscular belly. She heard his breath catch in his throat, and he whispered her name.

"Claudia?"

"Shhh." She reached up and touched her finger to his lips. His eyes widened in surprise when she captured his chin in her hand and lifted it, so that she could kiss him.

It was awkward at first, but it warmed swiftly as they found a sense of balance. He was trapped and unable to reach her, so she was in command. Her eyes drifted closed as she tasted his lips, marvelling at how wonderful it felt to kiss him when he was normal. No pheromones, no lightning bolts of pleasure — just him, and him alone. She was pleased to discover that sparks did still fly when she kissed him. Metaphorical sparks of genuine attraction, which drew her closer and closer until she was straddling his lap. With gentle hands, she caressed his cheeks and jaw, and helped him to keep his head up against the weight of the heavy collar. She could hear the soft clank as he strained against his chains, trying to embrace her, but he couldn't. He was helpless.

He was hers.

When their lips parted, she heard him gasping to try

and catch his breath, and felt the tremble of anticipation run all the way through his body. She traced her fingertips down across his chiselled chest, over his belly, and to the front of his trousers. Sure enough, she could feel the swell of his arousal through the cloth, and he gasped again at the touch of her fingers against swollen, sensitive flesh.

With a smile on her face, she eased herself back and slowly rose to her feet. His eyes followed her, watching her with longing, but he was at her mercy and they both knew it.

"Claudia…?" he whispered imploringly. "Please, don't tease me like this. I… I can't control my fertility right now. You could—"

He fell silent when her hands rose to the front of her blouse. One by one, she undid the buttons and slid the garment back off her shoulders. Her bra fell away a moment later. The sight of her bare breasts made him groan, but there was nothing that he could do. She drew out the moment out as long as possible and slowly slid down the zipper on her skirt, then she eased it off and let it fall in a heap at her feet.

Clad only in a light pair of briefs, she stepped forward again until she stood directly in front of him, filling his entire vision. His eyes roamed her hungrily, taking in the full curve of her breasts, the swell of her hips, the pert rosebuds of her nipples. She didn't have to look far to know that he wanted her. Desire was written across every aspect of his body, from the look in his eyes, the tension in his legs and torso, to the very obvious swell of his hard cock. He wanted her so badly that it almost hurt, and she could see it in his pained expression as he strained against his chains and made them rattle against the wall. When she finally slipped her thumbs into the waistband of her underpants and eased them down to leave herself nude, the sound of his groan made her shiver.

"Silly immortal," she replied, easing herself back down to straddle his thighs. He was not alone in his desire - she wanted him just as badly, and it was all she could do to control herself enough to keep from injuring him in her haste. Her fingers trembled on his zipper, making it difficult to grasp the tag, but she managed to ease it down without hurting him. "We mortal women have our own ways of protecting ourselves, you know. They're called long-term contraceptives; I'm surprised you haven't read about them."

Beneath his trousers, he wore a pair of simple black satin boxer shorts and she found herself oddly fascinated by the contrast in the textures. She ran her hand tenderly across the silky cloth, but then he moaned again and the feel of his hot breath across her skin made her forget all about fabrics. She looked up at his face and found him sweating and panting, his body trembling with lust. The desire to have him grew almost overwhelming, so she leaned in close and nuzzled his neck while her fingers slipped gently down the front of his shorts.

She felt his body stiffen when she finally touched his skin directly, and trailed a delicate fingertip along the length of his cock. Gently, she eased his manhood free, biting her own lip to try and keep her excitement at bay. But it wasn't to be; even without his hormones driving her crazy, she wanted him so very, very badly that she couldn't hold herself back.

With unladylike haste, she mounted him and guided his swollen girth into her body. They cried out in unison as she drove him as far within her as she could in a single, deep stroke. Her arms wrapped around his shoulders, drawing him close against her so that he could rest his head against her breast while she rode him, slow, hard, and deep.

His breath came in hot gasps across her, and even in the heat of passion she could hear him straining against the chains. He longed to touch her, to embrace her, to stroke her and kiss her everywhere, but he couldn't. He was trapped, and completely at her mercy. He still tried, though. All the way through, he was kissing her and nibbling her skin, doing what little he could to pleasure her.

Even without his gift to enhance the experience, she found herself growing closer and closer to climax. She ground herself on him, driving his cock so deep that it felt like she might explode. When her peak came at last, it hit her hard and fast; she threw her head back and screamed in pleasure, startling him with her cry. She clung to him as the throes of climax overwhelmed her, clutching him close against her writhing body.

Although he tried to control himself for her sake, without his powers to fall back on there was only so much one man could take. A few moments later, he joined her in exquisite ecstasy, his body jerking convulsively as he spilled his seed within her. Suddenly, she was kissing him again, and together they lost themselves in a world of the wonders shared only by two.

Neither of them really noticed the faint sound of stone turning to sand behind them, but they did hear the awkward sound of someone clearing his throat. Claudia jumped in surprise and glanced back over her shoulder, where she found Piotr in the doorway trying very hard not to look at them.

"Christ, can't we have a moment's privacy here?" she cried in protest. She snatched up her blouse from where it had fallen, to hastily cover her breasts. It was a feeble effort and completely pointless, since she was completely naked and still thoroughly mounted on Luke's fading erection, but she felt the need to do something to preserve her modesty.

"Sorry, sorry," Piotr rumbled, hiding his eyes behind his hand. "Have orders to fetch you both immediately. Cabal coming, must go."

"Turn around," Claudia snapped, and Piotr leapt to obey. Once his back was turned, she eased herself off of Luke and hurried to pull her clothes back on.

"Sweetheart, if you wouldn't mind?" Luke whispered to her as she was just finishing buttoning up her blouse, and then tilted his head down. She followed his eye to his exposed crotch and immediately understood. Fighting the unreasonable urge to laugh, she dropped back to her knees beside him to tuck his manhood back into his trousers, and then gently did up his fly. When she glanced up to check if she'd injured him at all, she found him smiling at her in a strange, adoring way.

Feeling unexpectedly shy, she smiled back and tucked a strand of hair behind her ear. She leaned forward to kiss him softly - but just at the moment their lips touched, the entire building trembled with the sound of a powerful explosive force. Claudia squeaked in surprise and jerked back, looking around frantically to try and figure out if that was somehow her fault. It wasn't, though. She could hear men cursing in several different languages, and the sound of gunfire overhead.

"Piotr?" she called urgently, their momentary embarrassment forgotten in the face of destruction from above. The huge man rushed back in and jogged over to them, where he began prying Luke off the wall. To her annoyance, she saw that he intended to bind her lover with his hands behind his back again.

Claudia reached out and grabbed Piotr's wrist. "For God's sake, just unchain him! He's not going to hurt anyone; he just wants to be with me."

As if to punctuate her sentence, a second explosion rocked their subterranean cavern, sending tendrils of dust oozing down from the ceiling all around them. Piotr hesitated for a second before he uttered something that sounded very much like a bad word in his native tongue, and fished a key out of his pocket.

The manacles clattered across the stone floor as they fell away, followed by the collar. Claudia hurried to help her lover to his feet, but as she got close to him his pheromones struck her like a drug, leaving her dizzy and lightheaded. Now that she knew what they were she could feel them quite clearly, but they didn't have the time to discuss it.

"Follow now, we go," Piotr ordered in broken English, and took off at a run. Luke stumbled as he took a step forward, struggling to convince his body to do what he wanted it to do after hours trapped in chains. Claudia tucked herself beneath his arm to help him keep his balance, and locked her arms around his waist. He shot her a grateful look, but there was no time to thank her, what with dust and pebbles raining down all around them.

Piotr drew further ahead of them with each step. Suddenly, Claudia realised he was leading them deeper into the earth, instead of towards the surface. With increasing frequency, explosions rocked the world above them. One struck so hard that it shook the tunnel and forced them to their knees. Claudia helped Luke scramble back to his feet, and they raced on with renewed urgency.

Suddenly, there was light up ahead. A moment later, they burst into an underground cavern, lit from above by some means she could not determine. Water filled the centre of the chamber, and in the pool a huge submarine bobbed patiently. There were several guards waiting for them, their hands resting on weapons ready to fight, but they relaxed when they recognised Piotr and the captives.

As they approached, she noticed that the guards were holding all their confiscated belongings. She was handed back her purse, coat, and both pairs of shoes, while Luke received his suit jacket, wallet, and belt. Before they had time to put their belongings on, a group of soldiers came rushing down the corridor behind them.

The last member of the group halted at the entrance of the cavern, and with a broad gesture of his muscular arms he drew on the Power to trigger the collapse of the passageway behind them. The entire cave quivered with the weight of the falling earth and stone. Startled by the display, Claudia panicked and clung to Luke, fearing that their cavern would be next.

Before she could properly recover, the soldiers began an orderly retreat to the submarine, and both she and her lover were swept along with them. She found herself aided by strong hands to climb onto the deck, and then helped down the ladder into the belly of the boat. Inside, they were guided to a cabin and told to stay there. Claudia was left stunned, clutching her purse and feeling completely out of her element.

"Wow." Luke stood beside her, absently scratching his chin. "I had no idea they had a submarine hidden down here. Even after a hundred years, you still see something new every day."

Claudia stared at him, totally bewildered, while she turned his words over in her mind. Then suddenly, something broke, and she dissolved into hysterical, uncontrollable laughter.

Chapter Ten

Once her brief bout of hysteria passed, Claudia settled down into a quiet, thoughtful mood. Although Luke sensed that she wanted to ask him questions, he was perfectly content to let her take her time working out what she wanted to ask.

After all, he had all the time in the world.

He watched curiously as she busied herself with personal grooming. She dug deep into her purse to fetch out a hairbrush, and attacked her lustrous white-blonde tresses with vigour. From his perspective, he couldn't work out what the problem was – he found her just as attractive with a head full of wild tangles as he did when she was immaculately coiffed.

When she caught him watching, she just gave him an embarrassed smile. He could only guess that it was a matter of comfort, because he could sense her relaxing as she went through the motions. Try as he might to suppress his bond with her, he could still feel the faint caress of her emotions against the edge of his psyche whenever they were close. If she was full of anger or lust, he felt the heat as if he were standing beside a furnace. When she was sad or distant, it felt icy and cold.

Now, as she was relaxing, he could feel the placid warmth like a soft blanket, calming him as well. They sat side by side on the edge of the narrow bunk in the cabin they'd been assigned to, close but not quite touching. The emotions radiating from her felt pleasant and soothing. He eased himself back to relax against the cabin wall and closed his eyes, just basking in her radiance.

"Are you reading my mind right now?"

Her words were petulant and demanding, but he could feel the humour behind them. When he opened his eyes again, he found her watching him, her body turned towards him with her long legs coiled up beneath her bottom.

"No," he said, closing his eyes again. "But I can feel what you're feeling. Your emotions affect me. Right now, you're feeling... calmer."

"What's it like?" she asked. Her tone was curious now, enquiring. A moment later, he felt the soft touch of inquisitive fingers upon his belly, and then the warmth of her body curling up against him. Her touch was soft and enjoyable, not entirely innocent yet not quite sexual either. He sensed that she longed for affection and closeness, and so he gave it to her without even thinking about it.

"It feels like standing beside the ocean," he replied, sliding his arm around her. The scent of her tickled his nostrils, but he was still satisfied from their brief tryst so for once it didn't overwhelm him. "Sometimes, it can be violent and overwhelming – like the raw power of storm-driven waves crashing against the shore. Sometimes it's smooth and calm, the water is warm and placid, stirred by just the lightest breeze that sends ripples skimming across the surface. That's what it's like right now."

"That's very poetic," she said, snuggling up against him.

He glanced down at her, uncertain whether she was mocking him or not, but there was no indication in either her thoughts or her body language that she was anything but serious. "Well, I've had a lot of time to think about it."

"I suppose you've had a lot of practice, too." This time, he felt a distinct echo of disquiet within her mind, like a pebble flicked across the glassy surface of a lake on a windless day.

"Not as much as you'd think," he replied, gathering her closer against him in an attempt to reassure her. When her eyes flickered open and looked up at him, he could see a mixture of disbelief and suspicion in them. "I don't usually let myself get close to people. I mean, I have had my share of sexual encounters, but mostly with women who treat it on a... professional basis, so there was no emotion involved."

"Whores? That's classy." She grimaced, and he could feel another wave of turbulence pass through her thoughts.

"Well, what choice do I have?" he said bitterly, frowning at her – he didn't much like the feeling of being judged. "If I let myself become emotionally involved with a mortal woman, then I will just have to watch her grow old and die while I remain young forever. The powers that be won't make someone immortal just because you love her. I already learned that lesson once. I still live with that pain every day."

He felt rather than saw her disquiet waver, replaced by a ripple of sympathy. "Oh... I'm sorry. I didn't know."

"It's all right," he reassured her, gently running his fingers through her soft hair. "How could you? It was a very long time ago. I met her during the war. She was a nurse. We fell in love, I proposed, and we agreed that we'd wed once the fighting ended. Unfortunately, before we could marry, my father revealed what he was and I was made immortal. He convinced me it was in her best interest to break her heart, so... I did."

"Why?" Claudia asked. "Surely if she really loved you, she would have understood?"

Luke opened his eyes and found her gazing up at him. There was no answer that he could give except the truth.

"Because I was young and stupid," Luke said bluntly. "I was seduced by tales of heroics and serving the greater good. I honestly thought what I was doing was committing my life to heroism, leadership, and preserving the civilized world. So I let my father use his contacts to convince her I died in the war." He hung his head, feeling shame as he always did when he thought back to his mortal life. "I didn't even have the courage to tell her the truth."

"You thought it would be kinder to let her grieve for you and move on, rather than leave her always wondering what she did to lose you," Claudia surmised, touching his hand sympathetically.

He closed his eyes and nodded. "She did. Maria went on and married someone else. Had a few children and lived happily ever after, without me in her life. She died thirty years ago surrounded by family and grandchildren, and never knew that I still loved her, and still watched over her as often as I could. And then you walked into my life, bold as brass, with your hair all done up in the exact same style she used to wear. How could I ignore that? It felt like a dagger in the heart, and a beacon of hope all at the same time."

Claudia stared at him thoughtfully but said nothing. She just let him speak and express himself, and Luke was grateful for it, because it was something he was rarely allowed to do.

"When I was first told about the plan, I expected you to be a vapid slip of nothing, raised to be servile and stupid," he said, tenderly touching her cheek. "When my father told me that you were anything but that, I was fascinated and worried at the same time. I wasn't sure if I had it in me to manipulate someone intelligent. Then I met you, and you were so beautiful, witty, and full of life. I actually *wanted* to be with you. The more I got to know you, the more repulsive the idea of using you became."

"And yet, somehow," she finished the monologue for him, a smile playing across her lips, "we ended up crammed together in the cabin of a submarine, wearing the same filthy clothing we've been in for several days now. We're being chased by people that want to shoot us or worse, and we're under the protection of people that don't really seem to care one way or another. Yet somehow, it's okay because we're in this together."

"Well, when you put it that way, it does seem a little ridiculous," he replied with a wry smile, absently rubbing the two days' worth of stubble that roughed his jaw.

"Or a little romantic, depending on how you look at it." She reached up to stroke one knuckle over the line of his jaw as well. "Is this how all immortals fall in love, or just you?"

"Just me, I think," he said, his smile turning embarrassed. "I have no idea if the elders can even feel love. It looks like they start to lose the little things that make us human as they get older, but they may just get better at hiding it. Either way, I'm glad to say that I'm not quite there yet."

***

"I'm relieved about that, too, otherwise I'd probably be dead by now." Claudia sighed and slipped her arms around his waist, snuggling up against his side. While she had almost taken offense at the beginning of the conversation, his explanation eased her tensions and soothed her fears.

Now that she understood him a little better, she saw that he was a man of principles and respect who put the needs of others above his own. They'd used him just as much as they'd tried to use her, and yet he still had the guts to stand up for her, even if it meant putting his own life on the line. That was something that she liked, a lot.

Resting her head against his belly, she closed her eyes and asked another question, to change the subject to something a little less emotionally intense. "Where do you think they're taking us?"

"Europe, I imagine," Luke replied.

"Europe?" Her eyes opened and she stared up at him, surprised. "But that's the other side of the world. I don't have any of my things, or my passport."

"Well, I'm just guessing, but it seems logical." He gave her a smile, and trailed his fingers along the curve of her cheek. "I wouldn't worry too much about your passport. The Immortelle rule every aspect of international affairs. If they want to take you to Europe, then you'll go to Europe and you'll get in with no trouble at all."

"But what about my things?" she asked, seeking guidance from his experience. "My clothing, my jewellery – my shoes? I didn't plan for any of this. I'm sure my mother will have my bank account frozen by the time we reach shore. What will I wear? Even Chanel will only put up with a certain amount of abuse before I start to look like a ragamuffin." She looked down at her rumpled suit sadly, and then flicked him another worried glance.

"Don't worry about it, love," he replied. He caught her chin with gentle fingers and tilted it up, distracting her with the warmth of his smile. "I've had plenty of time to make just-in-case emergency plans. We'll be fine."

"I'm not sure how I feel about relying on my boyfriend for financial support," she said, frowning deeply. She didn't quite realise what had slipped out of her mouth until she saw his eyes light up in unexpected delight. It took a moment before she realised that she'd accidentally referred to him as her boyfriend, and then her cheeks began to burn – but she made no attempt to rescind her statement.

"It's only for a short time, until you're better established," he replied, glossing over her slip of the tongue with great diplomacy. "If you end up joining the ranks of the Führung, then you will never have to worry about money again. They're the wealthiest of the Western clans."

"So I go from living on Mother's bankroll, to living on your bankroll, to living on my father's bankroll?" She made an unladylike noise and shook her head. "I just want to be financially independent, damn it!"

Luke laughed and leaned down to press the tenderest of kisses against her lips. "You'll get there. Just give it time. In the meantime, why don't we have a nap? I haven't slept in days."

"All right," she agreed readily, content to let him soothe her anxiety and distract her. Although she had managed to catch a few moments of rest throughout their ordeal, her body was complaining over the lack of solid sleep. Once the decision was made, they undressed awkwardly in their narrow chamber and hung their clothes in the cupboard that passed for a closet in the hopes that gravity might make them more presentable by the time they awoke.

The bed they shared was nothing more than a narrow cot, but neither of them really minded. By the time her head hit the pillow and she felt the warmth of Luke' arms slide protectively around her waist, Claudia was fast asleep.

***

For Luke, sleep took longer to arrive, but he was comfortable and content regardless. He nuzzled his face against the back of his Claudia's neck, enjoying the soft scent of her hair and skin. Her perfume was long gone, but he didn't mind – he found her natural scent even more appealing.

He'd longed for this moment since they'd first coupled, to spend a few hours curled up against her in blessed sleep. There was an intimacy to the act of sleeping beside another person far surpassed mere sex, as far as he was concerned. It took trust and affection, which was something he had deliberately withheld from himself to try and keep his sexual relationships free of emotion. Now, as he closed his eyes and snuggled against Claudia's back, he realised just how much he'd longed for trust over the years. It made everything feel worthwhile.

Chapter Eleven

The hours drifted by in their little cabin, but without daylight there was no way to mark the passage of time. Three times a day, they were brought food by the impassive guards who stood watch outside their door, and they had access to a tiny bathroom with a toilet and shower, so they were not uncomfortable. As prison cells went, this one was claustrophobic but not entirely unpleasant.

With little else to do, they spent their time talking, reading and making love. Claudia's seemingly bottomless purse contained an e-reader, which she had shared with Luke after he'd revealed that his body only required a few hours of sleep a night. While she rested, he lay beside her, reading quietly.

Their choice in literature varied greatly, but he found himself fascinated by the differences rather than frustrated. Her collection of books revolved around two things – the law, and love. All his life, he had scorned the idea of romance as a genre, and yet now he found himself enjoying the stories of courtship, sensuality, and passion.

More than once, he found himself becoming affected by the poetic words and the scent of his lover's closeness. Although he never deliberately woke her from her slumber, she often came awake on her own in response to his pheromones. Each time, she teased him about his reaction to her silly books, but passion swiftly overwhelmed them and her teasing was forgotten in the heat of the moment.

It was during one such interlude that a knock came on the door. They'd finished their indulgence a quarter of an hour before, and lay side by side in rest. Luke was awake but relaxed, laying on his back with one arm cast behind his head, staring off at nothing in particular as he languished in the afterglow. Claudia was napping again, her cheek resting against his chest and one slim arm cast haphazardly across his belly. She wasn't truly sleeping, just dozing and enjoying the warmth. Every so often she would move a little, curling a leg over his or trailing her fingers across his stomach. She'd swiftly learned his weaknesses, and was becoming quite adept bringing out his inner demon. He was already halfway aroused again by her subtle teasing, so he met the interruption with a disproportionate amount of annoyance.

"What is it?" he snapped at the door, as though it were the door's fault. Claudia stirred in his arms to draw the blanket up a little higher. Without even thinking, he found himself helping her, gently adjusting the blanket just so to help protect her modesty.

The heavy steel door creaked open, and Piotr ducked through. To Luke's amusement, he needed to bend almost double to keep from cracking his head on the door frame. Even more amusing was the glance he shot towards them. Luke didn't need to read minds to see the flicker of envy that passed across the big man's face.

Luke understood. Claudia was young and nubile, with the kind of generous curves that their generation relished. If their roles had been reversed, Luke would have been envious as well.

"We come to Australia in about an hour," Piotr rumbled, a flicker of annoyance passing across his face as he glanced away from them. "Then we go by plane."

"We'll be ready," Luke replied amiably. He and Piotr were of a like age and origin, so he considered the Polish Immortelle something of a friend, despite everything that had happened. His smile faded after a moment into a thoughtful frown, and then he appealed earnestly to the other man. "We need fresh clothing. Could you...?"

"I get," Piotr grunted, nodding sharply. The annoyance on his face faded, replaced by the kind of impish expression that Luke immediately sensed was trouble.

"Perhaps you could get one of the *female* members of your clan to arrange it?" he asked dryly, fighting to hide his amusement.

"Bah, you no fun." Piotr scoffed and waved a hand. "Fine, fine. We get proper clothing."

After the large immortal departed in a huff and the door closed behind him, Claudia opened one eye and looked up at Luke curiously. "Why do I feel like you just saved me from a fate worse than a neon yellow thong?"

"Because I did," he replied, chuckling. "And knowing him, it probably would have been a crotchless neon yellow thong, and something even worse for me."

"My hero," Claudia teased, teased, running her hand playfully up across his chest. "How long did he say we had, again? An hour?"

"Mhm, about that." He peered at her sideways, trailing his fingers thoughtfully across her shoulder. "Are you thinking what I'm thinking?"

Apparently, she was. Before the question was even out of his mouth, Claudia was straddling his waist with her hands on either side of his head, her golden hair forming a halo around her face that was anything but angelic.

"If you're thinking that's just enough time for a

quickie, then I absolutely am," she replied with a grin, and leaned down to capture his lips in a playful kiss.

His laughter was muffled by her affection, and by the heat that gathered swiftly in his loins. By the time she flicked her hair back over her shoulder and sat up straight to mount him, his manhood was ready and waiting for her.

"Mmrgh," he murmured inarticulately, savouring the delicious sensation as she teased him with her body. "I think we'll be pushing it to keep it under an hour."

Claudia laughed merrily, trailing her nails gently around the base of his cock as she eased herself down onto him. "Then I'll just have to figure out how to make you lose control a little faster than usual, won't I?"

In a moment, all coherent thought was blown away in the face of intense, frantic passion.

***

Three-quarters of an hour later, Claudia collapsed atop him, exhausted, her skin glistening with sweat. She felt a gentle hand cradling her, stroking her, guiding her through her climax with a tenderness that made it all the more intense. He joined her only once he was sure that she was satisfied, and once more she felt that glorious explosion of heat deep inside her.

No matter how many times they made love, it never felt any less intense. Although she'd had her share of men in her life, none of them made her tingle the way he did. As he gathered her up and rolled her onto her back to use the last few thrusts left in him to pleasure her as much as he could, she marvelled at the way having his seed inside her made her feel.

It was almost like a drug, addictive, super-heated,

permeating her entire body with a rosy glow that lasted for hours after climax. Her eyes fluttered closed and her back arched as she wrapped her legs around him, holding him within her for a moment longer before she could bear to let him go.

"How do you do that?" she groaned, reluctant to relinquish her grasp on him. He turned an inquisitive look up at her, in the midst of trailing his lips across her naked breast.

"Do what?" he asked, pressing a kiss to the crevice between her breasts. Then he was moving up along her body, trailing kisses across her collarbone to the side of her neck.

"You know... oh!" She gasped sharply and her eyes flew wide when he lavished a tender love-bite on the side of her throat, just hard enough to leave a small mark. "Ooh... ah, how do you— you know, most men need some down-time to recover..."

"Ahh." He made an amused little sound almost like a purr, his breath hot across her freshly-nibbled skin. "I was wondering how long it would take you to ask about that." He drew back and gazed down at her with a smile. "You remember how I mentioned that my biology was mutated by the elixir? An unlimited libido is one of the perks of that."

"Unlimited, huh?" She closed her eyes as he curled up over her again, trailing kisses all the way down her body this time. His hands stroked her skin, leaving a trail of tingling nerves across her waist, hip and thigh.

"They do liken me to a demonic sex-fiend for a reason," he replied, kissing his way down across her belly until his lips danced over the moist heat of her sex. His tongue darted out swiftly to tease her, drawing a gasp of surprise and pleasure from her, but it only lasted for a second before he eased himself back. "We have to get up now, love."

"Aw, must we?" she complained, stretching out languidly, just to tease him. Sure enough, she saw the flicker of interest dance through his eyes, but he drew a deep breath to steady himself and looked away.

"Sadly, we must." As hard as it was for both of them, he finally extracted himself from her embrace completely and stood up, then he offered her a hand in a gentlemanly fashion. She took it and rose, leaning up on tiptoes to press a kiss against his cheek.

"Pity that shower is too small for us to share," she said. She lingered against him for a moment before she finally slipped away and headed for the bathroom.

***

"Next time, my love." Luke turned to watch her go, studying the curve of her hips as she walked away. He knew that she knew he was watching, and that she was teasing him deliberately, but that didn't stop his body from responding to the sight of her, the smell of her — even the taste of her that still lingered on his lips.

Once she was out of sight, he blew a deep breath and ran his fingers back through his hair. It would definitely have to be a cold shower for him when his turn came around. A very, very cold shower.

***

Their departure from Melbourne took longer than expected, though no one bothered to inform either of them what the delay was about.

Shortly after they'd finished bathing and getting dressed, Piotr returned to usher them up to the surface.

Luke helped Claudia up the ladder and back onto solid ground, though she was nimble enough that she barely needed him. Still, it was the gentlemanly thing to do. Once they were ashore, they stood to one side and waited while the Führung raced around, getting ready for their departure.

For a moment, Luke felt vaguely uncomfortable. He'd gotten used to the incessant swaying motion while they'd been trapped in the submarine, but it only took him a few minutes to get his land legs back. They found themselves standing inside a building that looked like an aircraft hangar, if not for the fact that the entire middle of the room had been hollowed out and filled with water.

He felt Claudia's weight against his arm, but when he glanced at her he realised that she wasn't trying to get his attention. She was in the middle of shimmying back into her stockings, and using him to keep her balance while she did so. Through their bond, he sensed her need to look presentable, and felt her relaxing once she had her shoes back on. Her clothing might be crumpled and her hair uncurled, but at least she *felt* better, and that was the important thing.

Luke couldn't have cared less about what she was wearing, but he was content to let her do whatever she needed to do. He considered the stilettoes a ridiculous fashion trend, but... watching her wriggling into her stockings stirred him in ways he couldn't hope to verbalise. Such a simple thing shouldn't have been so erotic, and yet it took all of his strength not to bend her over the nearest table and have his wicked way with her right there and then, regardless of how many people were watching.

The worst part was that she had no idea how the

tiny nuances of her movement and dress affected him. He glanced at her again a few moments later, and caught her absently smoothing the fabric of her blouse across her flat belly, then tucking her hair back behind her ear while she watched the men around her at work.

The love-bite on her neck was quite visible, a tiny little bruise that marked her as his. Luke absently adjusted his own collar, and tried to focus his attention on the activity around them. The cold shower hadn't been enough to cool his incessant ardour, but at least he was clean. Such was the curse of the Cabalist.

Finally, he spotted Piotr approaching them, and was surprisingly relieved for the distraction.

"Come, come, we go," Piotr rumbled, beckoning for them to follow him. He felt Claudia's hand slip into his, and glanced down to find her smiling at him adoringly. Side by side, they followed in Piotr out of the hangar, her heels clicking in time with their progress.

***

The sunlight made Claudia blink as they stepped through the door. She could smell the unique scent of the red earth baking beneath the searing summer sun, and it was familiar if not altogether pleasant. She'd spent most of her life in Australia, though thanks to her mother it had never really felt like home. She had no friends to speak of, no family aside from her mother. Nothing that bound her to the land except for her accent – and Mother had tried to take that away from her, too.

A private jet waited for them. Before she could look around at all, she was being led up the stairs into the lavishly-appointed cabin. Luxuriant leather armchairs and couches waited for them, and the flight attendant that led them to their places was very formal and immaculately presented.

In crisp, flawless English with a heavy German accent, she directed them to a pair of small suitcases waiting in front of their seats. Claudia opened hers to find neatly folded clothing in a variety of styles, all tastefully selected with an eye for both comfort and fashion. To her relief, there was not a single sliver of neon yellow in sight.

"Thank you," she said to the flight attendant, who smiled politely and pointed her towards the ladies room at the rear of the cabin in return. Claudia selected a set of clean undergarments, pair of tan slacks, and a nice white blouse, then she retreated to the bathroom to change.

Without the aid of her favourite tools, there was only so much she could do with her hair. She brushed it until it shone, and pinned it up behind one ear with a small hair clip so that it curled girlishly around her cheek. With a touch of eyeliner, mascara, lip gloss, and her new clothing, she looked and felt like a whole new woman by the time she finally returned to the cabin.

Luke had already changed and was waiting in his seat, looking handsome in formal dress slacks and a black silk shirt that set off the colour of his eyes. He'd brushed back his hair from his forehead, but since he was lacking his usual hair products it looked more dishevelled than she was used to, a little wild and unkempt. As she eased herself into the seat next to him, she decided that she didn't mind at all – and judging by the appreciative look he gave her, her outfit met with his approval as well.

"Feeling better?" he asked. She nodded and gave him a shy smile in return, acknowledging without words that his intuition was right: her need to groom was deep-seated in her personality.

"We're still on the ground. Is there a problem?" she asked. She glanced around, but neither the flight attendant nor any of their guards were visible. "Where is everyone?"

"I have no idea." Luke shrugged and leaned over to stare out the window, searching for signs of life. "It was empty when I came out. I guess we have no choice but to wait."

"I swear, if we're going to get attacked again, I'm going to be very annoyed," she commented, only half-kidding. She winked at him playfully and set her purse down on the coffee table in front of their seats. On a whim, she pulled out her phone and switched it on. "Hey, we've got reception."

"Don't!" Luke spun back to her, and grabbed her wrist. She opened her mouth to protest, but whatever she was going to say died on her lips. Mere seconds after it had finished powering up and found reception, the phone rang in her hand. Both of them looked down, and stared at it in shock.

The call was from a number that they both recognised: it belonged to William Logan.

"Don't answer it," Luke hissed, his grip on her wrist tightening. Claudia shot him a look, then shook her head.

"I think I should. Talking is what I do best, you know." She drew a deep breath to steady herself, then answered the phone call and put it on speaker. "Hello, William. You have some nerve calling me, after what you've done."

"Hello, Claudia – and Luke, I presume." The voice on the other end of the phone was smooth, calm, and ever so slightly sensual. "I see you've made it to Australia. That's a pity."

"Oh, I'm sure it is. We're beyond your reach now," Claudia answered firmly. "I suppose you'll be following us, then?"

"No. You're too deep inside Führung territory now," he replied. "We of the Cabal are lovers and diplomats, not warriors. We rarely resort to violence. We've already tried that and it didn't work, so I'm calling you to try diplomacy. Come back to us, Claudia. We can make you happy here."

"You tried to kill me just a couple of days ago, and now you're asking me to come back willingly?" Claudia repeated, incredulous. "I thought you had some nerve calling me to talk, but this is a whole other kind of crazy. What could you possibly offer me that would make me think that's a good idea?"

"Whatever you want, Claudia," William replied, his voice deep and soothing, almost hypnotic. "Money. Power. Men – or women, if you prefer. We can give you anything. All we want in return is your child, and then we'll give you eternal happiness as a member of the Cabal. You don't even have to carry it to term, unless you want to. We could arrange a surrogate."

"Eternal happiness, like you did for me?" Luke said suddenly. Claudia glanced at him, startled by the bitterness in his voice. "The promises of the Cabal are laced with lies, Father. We all know that. It's what we do. Claudia wants to know where she comes from, so I'm taking her to meet *her* father. I think he'll do what you never bothered to, and actually treat her well. At least the Führung deal with honour!"

"Honour, son?" William's voice carried a note of anger that matched Luke's bitterness. "You betrayed me, and everything that you swore to protect. You've broken your vows and cast us aside for the sake of a woman. What would you know of honour? You're the last person in the world that has the right to lecture me about honour."

"Girls, girls, you're both pretty," Claudia interrupted, her tone dry and sarcastic. "Now, if you don't mind, I'd like a chance to respond to your offer."

Luke shot her a dark look, but William Logan merely took a metaphoric step back from the argument. "Yes, please do. Remember, we can offer you whatever makes you happy, Claudia. Anything. Eternity is a very long time."

"Anything? Really?" she replied. "Well, in that case... Fuck off, Bill. Solon. Whatever your name is. Just leave us the hell alone. You've already done enough damage, to both me and your own son. You've ruined whatever there could have been here. You destroyed it, spat on it, then kicked it into a sewer. If we ever choose to have a baby, then she'll be ours and you'll never even have the chance to meet her. Your own granddaughter. And you know why? Because you did this. You destroyed your own family for the sake of power. So, you just think about that, while you're enjoying your eternity all alone."

Without another word, Claudia terminated the call and switched her phone off. She shoved it back into her purse and glanced at Luke. He stared back at her with a look of open admiration on his handsome face.

"Have I told you how beautiful you are any time recently?" he asked.

"Not in the last five minutes, so please feel free to tell me again," she replied.

Luke chuckled softly and put his arm around her to give her a gentle squeeze. With his free hand, he scooped her chin up to give her a soft kiss, one so ripe with tenderness that she immediately felt the lingering anger from her conversation with his father fade. Her eyes fluttered closed as she melted against him, enjoying the warmth and closeness of his touch.

Someone cleared their throat nearby, and interrupting their moment. She glanced up and found Piotr standing over them. Like them, he'd changed his clothing and now stood resplendent in an exquisitely tailored grey suit. In spite of herself, Claudia was impressed. The big man cleaned up rather nicely. Not as nicely as Luke, but Luke did have an unfair advantage.

"No Mile High Club, please and thank you," Piotr rumbled, planting himself in a seat across the aisle. Behind him, various members of his clan filtered in and took their places. The hostess reappeared as if by magic from wherever she'd gone, and filtered down the aisle taking orders for food and beverages.

Claudia and Luke exchanged a glance that was equal parts amused and uncomfortable. Finally, after what felt like forever, they heard the soft rumble of the engine starting up. The hostess issued instructions for everyone to buckle up, then seated herself and did the same. A few minutes later, gravity pressed them back in their seats as the plane taxied down the runway and up into the air, carrying them away into the unknown.

Chapter Twelve

Claudia stared out the window at the changing landscape as the hours rolled by, her elbow resting on the edge of the window sill and her chin upon her palm. Luke had been content to switch seats with her mid-flight so that she could have the window, particularly after she'd revealed that this was her very first trip to Europe.

"You know when I was a girl, I always wondered why we never took holidays in Europe like all my friends at school," she said, her voice shattering the silence and drawing Luke's attention away from the book he'd been reading. "Mother always told me that she was simply too busy to take the time off work, but now I think I understand."

"Oh?" Luke queried, looking pleased rather than annoyed by the chance to let her talk through her thoughts. Anything for a break from the monotony. Even immortals got bored during long journeys, and he had admitted to her that he was no different.

"Well, it makes sense when you think about it," she said, as much to herself as to him. "She couldn't go to France, Italy or Spain, since that's your Cabal's territory and it would look suspicious. And she couldn't take me to Germany or any of those countries around there, or she would run the risk having the Führung find out about me. When you eliminate those countries, where else is there to visit? Russia? Not exactly a dream vacation, and you mentioned that the Slavic Immortelle are a bit odd so I'm guessing that 'odd' means 'dangerous'. I used to daydream about going shopping in Paris, or skiing in Switzerland, and I never understood why she wouldn't let me go."

"You go now," Piotr chipped in suddenly, his voice carrying a note of sympathy. They both looked over at him and found him watching them with a half-smile lingering on his lips.

"To Switzerland?" she asked. "I always wanted to see the Alps."

Piotr nodded vigorously and pointed towards her window. "You keep looking. Soon you will see. We are almost there."

Claudia obediently leaned over her window, but all she could see was the vibrant cerulean of the Mediterranean Sea. It was so beautiful that it lifted her heart for a moment, until reality brought it crashing back down. Somehow, Luke caught the sound of her sigh over the whine of the engine, and he reached out to touch her shoulder.

She glanced at him and gave him a faint smile. "Just thinking that now I'll never get to see any of the Cabal's countries."

"Never say never, my love," Luke replied reassuringly. "Your clan and mine were allies up until just before World War II. Allegiances change over time as treaties are forged and broken. One day, you may very well have the chance. But, on the plus side, your clan owns most of continental Europe as far north as Finland, down through most of Poland, and as far south as Macedonia."

"Greece now," Piotr said, his deep voice jovial and friendly. At some point during the voyage, he seemed to have decided that intimidating them was pointless, so he'd stopped trying. Like a big, blond puppy, he was much better at being playful than scary.

"You have Greece?" Luke asked, shooting a surprised glance at him. "I thought the Slavs had Greece?"

"No, nobody want Greece. Good resources, but poor government." Piotr snorted and shook his head. "We buy. We fix."

"Good luck with that," Luke replied, and then glanced at Claudia. She was confused by the banter and her expression must have shown it, because he took a moment to explain it for her. "Greece has been a political football for the past two millennia. We originally owned the territory, but we traded it to the Dragon Clans in the Far East at some point long before I was born. I have no idea why, but I'm sure it made sense at the time. Since then, it's changed hands a dozen times."

"Greece is like a whore," Piotr said. "Everyone want to look up her skirt, everyone like what they see, but when they finish their rut they grow bored with her and shoo her away." He thumped an enormous fist proudly against his chest, and gave them a smirk. "The Führung will make the whore into a lady again."

"A crude metaphor, but apt," Luke said, shooting him a long-suffering look, then he looked back at Claudia. "Maybe we should have let the Cabal have you after all, to keep you away from these barbarians."

"No, thank you," she replied, smiling at him. "You're the only one of them that I like."

"Is good choice," Piotr rumbled good-naturedly. "Kid is funny when he is drunk."

Luke sighed and shook his head. "I don't drink anymore, Piotr. Not after the last time."

"Bah, coward." A wicked grin twisted the big man's face. "I bet your girl can hold her liquor."

"Me?" Claudia squeaked. "Oh, don't you bring me into this. I still have a mortal liver, thank you very much. You'd probably both beat me."

Her comment brought an amused guffaw from Piotr and chuckles from the other guards, as well as a smile from Luke. Once the levity passed, she settled back down to stare out the window, waiting impatiently for the trip to be over.

***

Claudia was halfway through her fourth cup of tea when the jagged peaks of the Swiss Alps manifested as if by magic out of the rolling, snow-covered plains of Europe. Her breath caught in her throat as they rose in sharp relief against the azure arc of the sky.

Luke heard her gasp and leaned past her to get a look for himself. He'd never been to Switzerland either, so he found himself sharing a little bit of her awe. With gentle fingers, he confiscated her teacup before she could drop it, then took her hands and held them gently.

There was a chime when the seatbelts sign came on, distracting them for a moment. By the time his gaze returned to the window, the plane had banked to the right, and taken the Alps out of their line of sight. Now the Swiss highlands spread out in an endless patchwork blanket below them, the white of heavy snow interspersed with vibrant greens and blues. Luke felt Claudia's emotions as they came: the sight left her breathless, and she suddenly found herself feeling very small.

Luke held her gently, and let the swell of her emotions guide his. Their hearts soared together, and somehow he felt closer to the Power than he ever had before. A snippet of poetry came to him, and he leaned down to whisper the words in Claudia's ear. "'The immense mountains and precipices that overhung me on every side, the sound of the river raging amongst the rocks and the dashing of the waterfalls all around, bespoke of a Power mighty as Omnipotence.'"

Claudia shivered in his arms. He couldn't be sure whether it was the view that caused it, the poetry, or if she was starting to sense the Power's presence through him. The bond could be a two-way street, if they let it become one – and Luke had never received the training he needed to stop it.

But I don't have to stop it, he realised suddenly. He could feel her need for closeness, and understood without words that she wanted the bond. He took a deep breath and relaxed, opening himself up to her as best he knew how. Together, in contented silence, they watched the might of the world unfold beneath them, and together they endured the overwhelming sense of smallness that the mountains brought to the hearts of human beings. To both mortals and immortals alike, the mountains seemed like the handiwork of the gods alone.

***

Half an hour later, their plane finally banked in to land, swooping down between two jagged peaks in a dramatic moment that made Claudia panic, until she realised that the peaks concealed a tiny runway. The jet touched down safely on the frigid tarmac and taxied to a halt, but she could see little through the frost on the window.

Even through the shell of the jet, she could feel the frigid cold. She reached for her suitcase, and was relieved to find a warm sweater and jacket inside it. Then she glanced at Luke, and was surprised to see him bundling up as well. He caught her glance and gave her a wry smile in return.

"I may be immortal, but I'm not immune to the cold," he said. "At least, not like they are."

He tilted his chin towards Piotr. The enormous man flashed a salute and a half-smile, then took both of their suitcases and stepped out into the cold without any sign of discomfort whatsoever. Claudia shouldered her purse and followed after him, but unlike the European immortal, she shivered even with her winter gear.

Luke helped her down the slippery metal stairs to the tarmac, his hands gentle and attentive. When they were back on solid ground, he opened his heavy coat and drew her beneath it, snuggling her in against his body warmth. Although she felt a bit like a baby penguin in designer shoes, she accepted the offer without complaint. Luke's body practically radiated heat, and as she pressed up against him she found that her shivering eased.

The wind blew like the very breath of winter itself across the mountains. Piotr and his soldiers guided them over the tarmac, towards a door set directly into the side of the mountain. Unlike the ones she'd seen before, this one had an ordinary set of hinges and a heavy lock. A moment before the first members of their group reached the door, it swung open from within.

A small group of people waited just inside, led by a tall, dark-haired woman who might have been stunningly beautiful, if her expression hadn't been as cold as the air around them. Her hair was swept up into a harsh bun, highlighting her sharp cheekbones and high, angular brows. She was dressed in a tailored, dark grey suit jacket, pencil skirt, paired with dramatic stiletto heels.

The moment Claudia stepped through the door, she knew she was being assessed. It was a basic, animal thing, an understanding. With a single, sweeping glance, the woman took in every aspect of Claudia's appearance, from her hair to her clothing, and then it finally alighted upon her shoes. There, the woman's gaze lingered for a moment, and there was the slightest twitch of a sculpted brow.

The woman turned without a word and beckoned for them to follow her. As she did, Claudia glanced at the stranger's feet and spotted the tell-tale flash of a Louboutin-red sole, and knew instinctively that this hard-faced woman was a kindred soul. Luke glanced at her curiously, clearly sensing that there was something going on that he'd missed.

She just smiled and slipped her arm through his, and then led him off after the mysterious woman. Once the stranger was far enough ahead that she was out of earshot, Claudia leaned close to him and playfully whispered in his ear. "She's wearing French shoes. Should we be afraid?"

Luke shot an amused glance at her, then chuckled and shook his head. "My love, the Cabal owns about eighty percent of the world's fashion houses. Just because she wears quality, doesn't make her a threat – even if Monsieur Louboutin is a Cabalist Elder."

"He is?" Claudia gasped.

"Of course," Luke replied with a mysterious smile. "Do you really think it's possible to acquire that much skill in one short human lifespan?"

"I don't even know any more," she admitted. Her shoulders sagged, but Luke was quick to buoy her up, wrapping a supportive arm around her.

"Just think of this as an opportunity," he said. "Think of all the things you'll have the time to see and do and learn. When I was your age, I was sure the world would end before the turn of the millennium, and now look where we are. Just think of where this world could be tomorrow – and you could help guide them."

"Isn't that exactly what your father said to you?" she said dryly, giving him a long, sideways look.

"Well, yes," Luke admitted. He chuckled and shrugged sheepishly. "But he also failed to mention that the only thing the Cabal leads the world in is fashion and sex. The Führung are different. They're the most organised of all the clans except possibly the Dragons in the east. All the latest breakthroughs in medicine, science, and technology come through one of those two."

"Ooh, you make me blush," Piotr rumbled from behind them. His silly comment drew a giggle from Claudia, and Luke shot him an amused glare.

"Seriously, though," Luke said. "Of all the western clans, this one is the one that does the most good for humanity as a whole."

"But, you want good vibrator?" Piotr said. "Then, you go to Cabal."

This time, everyone laughed.

***

The dark stone passageways seemed to go on forever. Claudia's heels clicked in time with the woman leading them, but other than that the group had finally fallen into silence. After a dozen flights of stairs and what felt like a kilometre or more of tunnels, her feet were beginning to hurt. She was just trying to catch her breath enough to mutter a joke when they suddenly arrived at their destination.

Without any kind of warning, the tunnel they were in opened up into a massive chamber. The roof rocketed upwards into a dome, adorned with exquisite, multi-tiered chandeliers. The walls were decorated with tapestries and paintings that looked to be hundreds of years old, and the furniture was all plush purple velvets and rich, dark hardwoods.

But it was the view that made Claudia gasp. Beyond massive glass windows that stood three times taller than her head, the world opened up in a stunning, unobstructed vista. A single man stood silhouetted against the sunlight that practically glowed off the fresh-fallen snow, but Claudia didn't even see him.

She dragged Luke towards the windows. Together, they stood awe-struck by the beauty of the alpine lands. Below their mountain retreat, a snow-covered vale sprawled for miles, filled with old pine trees and tiny, picture-perfect buildings. It was the dead of winter, so snow covered every inch of the valley in a blanket of white, but that didn't matter. If anything, it just seemed more magnificent for it, so pristine and impossibly flawless.

"It's so beautiful," she whispered breathlessly. They were almost a kilometre above the valley floor, and it felt like she could see for an eternity. Tiny figures and vehicles moved far below, but from that height they looked like toys. The sun was beginning to set, and it cast long shadows across the valley, edging everything in shades of gold and pink.

"I am rather fond of the view, myself," the solitary stranger said. His voice was unexpected, and jolted Claudia out of her daze. It was a voice that she knew and had heard before, though not one she considered familiar yet. She looked to her left, and beside her stood the man she'd only met in a video conference before: the man Luke told her was her father.

In person, he was not as overwhelmingly large and all-powerful as he had appeared on that enormous monitor. He stood around three inches past six feet tall, and while his shoulders were broad he was not nearly as physically imposing as Piotr was. Yet, there was something about him that spoke of power.

Perhaps it was the eerie sense of calmness that he radiated, as though the world bent to his whim. Perhaps it was his eyes, which were a rare and curiously intense shade of turquoise. Claudia couldn't quite tell exactly what it was, but she was inclined to treat him with caution and respect. The two stood regarding one another for a while, each assessing the other but not quite sure how to react just yet. In the end, it was Claudia who broke the silence.

"Well, you certainly look like my father," she said. "But I suppose a DNA test is the only way we'll know for certain."

The High Elder nodded and snapped his fingers. The woman who had led them inside stepped forward from where she'd been waiting in the wings.

"That is why I am here, Miss Bell," she said. Her voice was a soft purr made elegant in a crisp European accent. There was a click as she set a little metal box down on a nearby table, and then she drew on a pair of sterile rubber gloves. Claudia understood immediately, and began removing her coat.

By the time the woman was ready to take her blood sample, Claudia's sleeve was rolled up, ready and waiting. She didn't flinch when the needle penetrated her skin, just held still and waited patiently. A little prick, and then it was over. The lady doctor pressed a small sticking plaster over the wound, and then she took the blood sample and departed through a side door.

Silence descended while the group waited. Claudia slid her coat back on again to combat the cold. Although the castle showed many modern conveniences, it was obviously designed for people who were immune to the chill. Without her coat, she swiftly found herself shivering again.

Although he looked uncomfortable in the presence of her father, Luke tucked her beneath his arm again and guarded her quietly against the creeping cold. Together, they watched darkness slowly embrace the world outside as the sun sank below the horizon.

The minutes stretched out until they felt like hours. Claudia felt anxiety building, but carefully calmed herself using the meditative techniques her mother had taught her. Now that she knew Luke shared in her emotions, she wanted to be more self-aware, since she didn't want to cause him any discomfort or distress.

His presence was soothing and warm, and he helped her to keep calm without saying a word. At one stage she caught him looking at her, but he simply smiled and touched her chin, and that was enough. There was an understanding between them, and that understanding kept her sane.

Suddenly, a door opened and then came the sharp click-clack of heels across the stone towards them. All three of them turned towards the source of the sound, and watch as the woman crossed the room to join them.

Claudia glanced towards the man that might be her father, and saw the faintest glimmer of anxiety on his face. No one else would have noticed it, but she was trained to see the signs. It reassured her a little, to know that he was just as worried as she was.

"Edler Herr," the woman said softly but clearly. "The test results are conclusive. This young woman is your daughter."

"How conclusive?" Gunther asked immediately, his voice cool and difficult to read.

"The test shows a 99.9999% match," she replied, keeping her expression carefully blank, and her words calm and even. "A more conclusive match is not possible. She *is* your daughter."

"Thank you, Helena," Gunther replied. "You may go."

The woman bowed her head respectfully and departed, leaving Claudia and Luke alone with the leader of the Führung clan. He turned and stared at Claudia, and for the first time she saw uncertainty written openly across his face. On instinct alone, she disentangled herself from Luke's embrace and stepped forward, to confront her father for the first time with any real certainty.

"So, now we know for sure," she said softly, drawing on every moment of her training to keep herself calm. "But, neither of us really knows how to deal with this. I've spent my entire life searching for my father, trying to figure out why he abandoned me, but now I've found out that he didn't. He – you – just never knew that I existed." She drew a deep breath to steady herself and then continued. "My mother did a terrible, unforgivable thing. I know that, and I'll understand if you want nothing to do with me. But I also hope that you can see I've done nothing wrong. I didn't even find out until a few days ago. I want absolutely nothing from you except the opportunity to make you proud of me."

"This is... an unexpected thing," Gunther replied. He stared at her, a troubled look playing across his glacial features. Claudia understood, and reached out to touch his hand softly, trying to reassure him the way only a daughter could. His skin was cold as ice to the touch, but he didn't withdraw.

"It's okay," she said with a smile. She released his hand and stepped back, returning to Luke's side. "Take as much time as you need. We'll leave you be, and give you some space. I understand that you need time to think. If you want to talk, I'm sure I'll be around here somewhere."

Then, without waiting to be dismissed, she took Luke by the hand and led him out of the room, to leave her father to mull over the decisions he needed to make in peace.

Chapter Thirteen

Fresh-fallen snow crunched softly underfoot as the couple made their way, hand in hand, through the tiny village nestled at the base of the mountains. Claudia shivered, and yet it was a delighted sort of shiver. Everything around her was so different, so wonderfully alien, and she loved every aspect of it – even the cold. To someone who had spent her entire life in the merciless heat of Australia, the contrast and newness of it all was fascinating.

After they'd left her father's presence the night before, they had found Piotr waiting for them. When she had told him the results of the DNA test, the big man's eyes had lit up and his entire demeanour softened. Suddenly, she was being treated as an honoured guest. Luke was respectfully tolerated, but even mere tolerance was better than being put back in chains again.

Piotr had guided them to a heated guest room, and their belongings had been brought to them there. Once they were settled in, the big man had invited them to dine with him in the castle's massive kitchens. Dinner had been delicious, cooked by the very best chefs and served by smiling wait staff who had tried very hard to speak English for her sake. After dinner, she and Luke had retreated to bed and slept until dawn woke them.

Claudia had awoken feeling rested and energetic,

and anxious to explore the exciting new world she'd found herself in. To Luke's delight, she'd decided to begin their morning with a quick, playful tussle that left them both feeling revitalised and happy. Once they extricated themselves from bed, they'd bathed, dressed, and – with the help of a passing servant – tracked down Piotr. Claudia had appealed to him to let her go explore the town, and he'd readily agreed.

Shortly thereafter, they were on their way down the mountainous roads in the back of a taxi. Claudia had barely been able to contain her excitement, and her enthusiasm rubbed off on Luke. Together, they'd explored tiny designer boutiques and shopped on his secret Swiss bank account. She invested in a pair of boots better suited to the weather, and they'd both purchased new clothing to replace what had been left behind. They stopped for breakfast in a tiny café overlooking the mountains, and marvelled at the way the castle high above them seemed to spring directly out of the living rock.

Now, they walked side-by-side through a frosty park. In one hand, Luke held a bundle of shopping bags; in the other, Claudia's gloved hand. He didn't mind the weight of the bags at all, because her presence buoyed him up and made it all worthwhile. It had been so many years since he'd had a lady to call his own that he would have done anything to make her happy. Lugging around a few shopping bags was the least he could do.

"It smells so different up here," she said suddenly, and paused to draw in a deep lungful of the crisp mountain air. "It's so clean and fresh. Everything is just... so beautiful!" In a moment of childlike delight, she released his hand and pirouetted away from him, her new winter boots crunching across the snow.

Luke smiled as he watched her dance with that pure, innocent human joy which delighted him more than anything else in the world. Her exuberance made him feel young again, as if all the years he'd survived before she was born had been spent waiting for the moment when he could be with her at last.

Suddenly, she grabbed his wrist and dragged him into her silly dance, and he was happy to let her. He let their bags fall away and swept her up into his arms, holding her close as they twirled together beneath the snow-laden trees. Overcome by a sudden fit of romantic whimsy, he hooked his arm around her waist and bent her over backwards.

He heard her gasp in surprise, and in his heart he felt a surge of victory – and longing. While he had her completely at his mercy, he kissed her deeply, slowly, and passionately, and let her feel the overwhelming emotion that she stirred within him.

***

Claudia was stunned for a moment. No one had ever kissed her like that before, not with such intensity and with such adoration. It felt like a moment from a movie, and she was the heroine. They had overcome all of the odds to be together, and this was their victory kiss. It was also a moment of trust, with him supporting her weight entirely, and she let him because she understood that he would never willingly let her come to any harm.

That kiss, it felt like it lasted forever and she was glad for it, because she never wanted it to end. Whether it was his pheromones or her own feelings, she truly didn't care, because that kiss was the only thing that mattered to her in the entire world. After what felt like an eternity, they both had to come up for air. She heard Luke gasping for breath, but it was a moment longer before she could bring herself to open her eyes and look up at him. When she did, she found herself all but hypnotised by his vivid, blue-eyed gaze, which was focused on her with such adoration that she could hardly believe such an expression could be targeted at her.

And yet, it was.

"Would it be too soon to ask you to marry me?" he asked. His voice was deep and husky, barely audible over the birdsong in the frosty trees all around them.

Her heart skipped a beat. "I— what? Marry you?"

"Well, it seemed like an appropriate moment," he admitted, a shy smile dancing across his lips.

"But we barely know each other!" she stammered, confusion and desire hammering at the edges of her mind. "It's only been two months."

"So it is too soon, then?" His smile didn't fade away, though it did twitch around the edges with barely-hidden amusement. With a gentleness that belied his strength, he eased her back to her feet, but still they stood together, enveloped in one another's embrace. "I have no concept of these things anymore."

"Yes, it's too soon, but I'm still flattered," she said, recovering her wits enough to give him a smile. At first it was a little awkward, but as she gazed up into those intense blue eyes, she felt herself relaxing again. "And I'm not saying no. I just need some more time."

"Good." He leaned down to touch his lips to hers, briefly and softly, just a whisper of a kiss. "Time is something we should have plenty of. Once you're one of us, we'll have all of eternity to spend together."

"There's no guarantee they'll even offer me the Immortelle," she said, then paused for a moment to think. "Is that the correct usage of the word?"

"Not entirely, my love," he replied, his eyes dancing with mirth. "'The Immortelle' is merely a collective noun used to describe my species. It is a play on words, referring to a species of flower that never fades even once it is picked. We are rendered immortal by an alchemical concoction that goes by any number of names. The Elixir of Life, the Draught of Eternity, or most often just The Elixir."

"Ah." She made a soft sound of understanding and nodded. "So, the flower has nothing to do with the elixir?"

"I have no idea," he admitted with a sheepish shrug. "Only the highest ranking members of each clan have the knowledge to make the elixir. It's how they stay in power. They literally bear the knowledge to propagate our species."

"Are you even truly human anymore?" she asked. To her relief, he didn't seem to take offense.

"I don't think so, no," he replied. "I am no master of the sciences, but I believe that what the elixir does is fast-forward evolution. We are to you what you are to Neanderthals." He gave her a quirky smile, and absently trailed a finger through her hair. "That sounds arrogant, doesn't it?"

Claudia just laughed. "I've seen you freeze grown men in their tracks just by looking at them. I've seen Piotr's soldiers turn stone to sand with the power of their mind. I've seen that castle up there," she gestured towards the distant fortress where her father's kin resided, "a building that looks for all the world like it grew out of the side of the mountain. Yes, it is arrogant, but it's deserved arrogance because it's the truth."

"I want you to become one of us," Luke said sudden, drawing her up hard against him. The tone of his voice changed so sharply that it took her by surprise. "I can't bear the thought of watching you die one day, and my species needs you. We *have* become arrogant, and we are the lesser for it. You could open their eyes, like you opened mine. Help bring the humanity back to the Immortelle, who have forgotten what it even means to be human."

"I don't understand," she admitted, staring up at him in confusion.

"No, I suppose you can't." Luke sighed heavily and released her, then gave her a faint smile. "My people have become wicked, my love – that is the honest truth. They take human lives as though they mean nothing. They've forgotten that they were once human as well, and that while we have supped upon the power of the gods, we are still only men."

"How could I possibly help with that? I am – pardon the pun – only human." Claudia reached out and took his hand, enveloping it with both of her own. Even with the gloves separating them, his warmth comforted her.

"To be honest with you, I have no idea," he replied. He lifted his free hand to run his knuckle softly along the curve of her jaw. "When we embraced that first time, I saw deep into your heart. I saw your potential for greatness. Your gift is not merely the power to shape mountains – it is your resilience, your kindness and your humanity. With time, I think you could become the best of us, and that might just be enough."

She smiled and shook her head slowly. "But I'm not even one of you yet."

"You will, if you want to be. Your father just needs time to accept you, and he will. He'd be a fool not to, and he's no fool." Luke slid his arms around her and drew her close, cuddling her in against his perpetual warmth. He always seemed to be a few degrees warmer than a normal person, but this far up in the Alps that was definitely a benefit rather than a curse.

"You make it sound like I'm going to be given a choice," she said dryly, nuzzling her face against the side of his neck. "But you're the one who taught me that choice is merely an illusion."

"I was wrong," he said, closing his eyes as they cuddled together to combat the cold. "I always thought that was the case, but I was wrong. I chose to leave everything I knew in the hopes that I could spend the rest of my eternity with you. When I made that choice, I was certain I would die for it, and yet..."

"...here we are, somehow still together and still alive," she finished his sentence and drew back to look up at him. "I think we're even on our first official date."

"What? Date?" Luke asked, confused. "Does it even count as a date if we're already sleeping together?"

"Of course it does!" she scolded him teasingly. "This is the modern age, old man. Goodness me, you are behind the times."

"I am, aren't I?" Luke heaved a sigh, but Claudia was swift to intercede before he could fall into moping.

"I was teasing you, silly," she said. She stood up on tiptoes to plant a kiss upon his lips, and then took him by the hand. "Come on – let me show you how we mere mortals date in this century."

***

The rest of their day was spent in child-like play, exploring the winter wonderland that surrounded their new alpine home. They spent their morning building snowmen and flinging snowballs at one another with energetic disregard for propriety, until they were chilled to the bone and had to retreat inside to warm up.

By lunchtime, they were huddled around a warm fireplace in a tiny restaurant, drinking soup from giant mugs and eating hot stew with freshly-baked bread. The conversation revolved around nothing, just books they'd read and authors they enjoyed. The more they spoke, the more Claudia realised that they had so much in common.

Despite his good looks, Luke was an intellectual at heart. He loved to read, to invest himself so completely in a book that it devoured his waking thoughts. He enjoyed practicing law for that same reason – that he could wrap himself up in a problem to the exclusion of all else, and turn it over and over, examining it from every angle until a solution finally presented itself. He was a very organised and analytical sort by nature, rarely as impulsive and demanding as the man Claudia had seen recently.

That was her fault, she discovered. Her spontaneity brought out his impulsive side, but when it came down to it they were just two sides of the same coin. Like him, Claudia loved to read and took great glee in solving a problem, but her method of attack was more aggressive. While his means to an end was to circle the problem and stare at it until a solution presented itself, she would poke it and prod it until she created a solution for herself.

"Maybe you should try writing," she suggested as they sat together in a little private room, watching deep purple-grey clouds gathering on the horizon. As the afternoon progressed, the weather had begun to change. Luke absently rubbed his neck and shrugged.

"It's going to snow again soon," he said to himself, then he glanced at her. "Maybe. I did think about it, but I'm not sure I would be a very good writer."

"Why not?" Claudia asked, sensing uncertainty behind his response. "You certainly have the life experience for it, not to mention the time."

"True, but I don't have much of an imagination," he admitted sheepishly.

"Oh, that doesn't sound like you at all." She narrowed her eyes, and gave him a pointed look.

"Hey, imagination in bed and imagination in writing are two completely different things," he replied. He laughed, and reached over to grab her around the waist, tugging her into his lap. "But... maybe I should try it. I do seem to be out of a job, and Cornelius Pharmaceuticals is unlikely to take me back now."

"Me either," she said, nodding her agreement. "I think we've royally messed up our resumes for the next few decades."

"Oh, it's not that bad. Everyone needs a lawyer at some stage or another. I'm sure your father will find a use for us." Luke smiled down at her, but his levity faded when her brows knitted into a frown. "What's wrong, Claudia?"

***

"Just thinking." Her frown deepened to the point that Luke felt a sudden stab of concern. Suddenly, her gaze flicked up to him, and she asked him a question that took him completely by surprise. "Does it hurt?"

"Does what hurt?" he asked, confused.

Claudia glanced around furtively, but the room they

were in was a small, private dining room just for two, and their waitress had left them in peace long ago. She rose swiftly from his lap and went over to close the door, then returned to stand in front of him. "Taking the elixir. Becoming another species. Does it hurt?"

"Oh." Luke sat back, and lowered his gaze thoughtfully to the ground. "I think it depends on the person. Everyone is different, and every clan has its own rituals. I know amongst the Slavs, there's a lot of screaming and knife-waving and blood-letting. I don't know about the Führung. They're very private people."

"Well, what was it like for you?" Claudia asked, easing herself back down into his lap. She closed her eyes and nestled in close, snuggling her head in beneath his chin. Luke drew a deep, thoughtful breath as her soft curls settled against his throat.

"For me... no, it didn't hurt. But it was very uncomfortable," he admitted, gently sweeping a strand of her hair away from her cheek and tucking it behind her ear. "But I'm not Führung. We're like different ethnic groups of the same species, in a way. My people have great powers over the mind, yours do not. I may have felt pain and had it erased from my memory afterwards."

"It was full of sex, wasn't it?" she said dryly. He sighed heavily and nodded. There was no polite way to say it, but he'd learned better than to try and keep secrets from her.

"All right, well, if you really want to know." He paused and shot a glance at her, as though he might get lucky and she'd have changed her mind. She didn't, of course. She just nodded firmly and gestured for him to continue. "I was drugged out of my mind first – opium, I think, but I'm not really sure – and then I was chained to a table. I vaguely remember a lot of chanting and mumbo-jumbo. You know, the usual secret society nonsense. There was an oath, something about eternal loyalty that I clearly didn't pay much attention to. The next thing I know, they're tipping this foul-tasting concoction down my throat. I remember choking and gagging, but they wouldn't let me throw it back up. Then I passed out."

"And?" Claudia urged, curiosity written all across her face. "What happened when you woke up?"

"Well, it's kind of a blur," he said quietly; suddenly, he found it difficult to make eye-contact with her. "I wasn't really sleeping so much as in a fever-state. From what I've heard from others who attended my initiation, I tossed and turned a lot. When I woke up fully, I was covered in bruises. I felt like I was on fire, like everything was all wrong and all so very right at the same time. I remember being hungry – ravenously hungry – both for food and for... other things."

"You know, you're the coyest incubus I've ever had the pleasure of meeting," she said, poking him playfully in the ribs.

"And if you keep interrupting, you're not getting the rest of the story," he replied, giving her a stern look. She muffled a giggle behind her hand and gestured for him to continue. "Right, as I was saying... when I woke up strapped to that table, I was half out of my mind. The drugs were still in my system so I wasn't all there, if you know what I mean. I was absolutely starving and so aroused that I couldn't think straight. I remember seeing the women come in – at least a dozen of them, maybe twenty – the Cabal's females in every shape and size. I didn't even care what they looked like. I was like a caged animal, totally out of control. That was the first time I caught the scent of a female as an Immortelle, and it drove me absolutely wild. They knew what would happen, and that's why they'd volunteered. I was a piece of meat to them, something new, young, and virile. A fun plaything for them to torment."

He cast a sheepish glance at Claudia, only to find her watching him with fascination. Embarrassed, he glanced away again. "They took their turns with me. Sometimes even two or three at a time. In between fucking me and tormenting me, they fed me red meat, bloody and barely cooked. I vaguely remember other men being there, but mostly they just stood back and watched. Then towards the end, when I was almost exhausted, they joined in. Not on me, I mean – on the women. That's when the orgy began in earnest, while I was still chained to the table. Panting, sweating, and sprawled out naked like a sacrifice on the altar. It was only then that I started to regain my senses, and realise what I'd done. What I'd become."

***

Luke drew a deep breath and closed his eyes. To her surprise, Claudia noticed a sag in his shoulders and the faintest ghost of a frown tugging at the corners of his lips. While she was enjoying his juicy little tale, she suddenly realised that he was not.

"You're ashamed," she said, her voice was soft as a whisper. His frown deepened, confirming her suspicion.

"As well I should be," he answered gruffly. "Just look at me. They call me an incubus. I'm a pervert, I thrive on sex. Before all this happened, I had one lady love and I treated her right. I was a gentleman."

"Oh, Luke," Claudia said, reaching up to touch his

cheek. "You're still a gentleman. Incubus or not, I've never had a man treat me as well as you do. Well, excluding that one time you addled my brain, but I understand why you did that."

"You deserve better than me," he whispered, softly and sadly. Claudia stared at him, her heart doing somersaults in her chest at the sight of him looking so sad. She only had one choice of action, and so she took it firmly and without hesitation, for his sake. She drew back her hand and smacked him soundly on the shoulder.

"Ow!" he yelped. "What the hell was that for?"

"Don't you ever say that again," she scolded, shaking a finger at him. "Not ever. Do you understand me?"

"Good Lord. Yes ma'am," he said, feigning fear. The blow hadn't been hard enough to do any damage or even really hurt, but it got the point across and snapped him out of his dark mood. "No need to resort to spousal abuse, woman."

"Go ahead and report me, then," she replied. "I'm perfectly happy to do the time if it keeps you from moping. Besides, last time I slapped you, you said you liked it."

"Well, yes," he admitted, a smile suddenly tugging at his lips. "But you weren't slapping my face..."

"You want me to aim a little lower?" she teased.

"Maybe," he replied, "but we probably shouldn't be doing that in public."

"Why don't we head home, then?" she suggested.

Luke grinned. "I think that's the best idea I've heard all day."

Chapter Fourteen

Claudia paced nervously, her pulse pounding in her ears. This was the moment of truth, and the one time when Luke couldn't be by her side to support her. A week had passed since her confrontation with her father, but now, finally, she had been summoned.

Luke waited with her in the antechamber, holding her hand and trying in some way to reassure her, but her nerves were getting the better of her.

"Calm down," he said, but she wasn't really listening.

"Are you sure my hair's okay?" she asked for the umpteenth time. Luke sighed in exasperation. Suddenly, he grabbed her and turned her to face him, then gave her a very gentle shake.

"Stop it," he commanded. "You look amazing. Your hair is perfect, your makeup is flawless, and for the last time no, your shoes are not 'too much'. Just... calm down. Please."

Claudia tensed up, fully prepared to take offense to his manhandling ways, but logic intervened. The truth was that his words were exactly what she needed to hear. She did look good, and she knew it. Her hair was immaculately groomed into the graceful vintage curls that she preferred, and her favourite suit was freshly dry-cleaned and pressed. Her heels were polished, her lashes were plumped, and she'd even found her favourite shade of lipstick in the local pharmacy: aptly named, 'Red Passion'.

"Oh for goodness' sake, listen to me going on and on." Claudia sighed heavily and smoothed an imaginary wrinkle from the front of her suit. "I'm sorry, Luke. I'm being an idiot. Anyone would think I was a silly little slip of fluff on her way to the debutante ball."

"It's all right, sweetheart." Luke smiled indulgently and slipped his arms around her waist, careful not to disturb her outfit. "I was just as nervous as you are when I first met the elders. I do understand. Just remember, you're a lawyer. You're calm, confident and self-assured. They're the jury, and you're the prosecutor."

"Shouldn't I be the defence?" she asked, flicking him a curious look.

"Oh God, no. You're the prosecution," Luke replied, shaking his head firmly. "Don't give them the slightest impression that you're begging. You must go in there with all guns blazing, and demand your birth right. That's how you'll impress them." He paused for a moment, and then gave her an encouraging smile. "That's how you impressed me."

"I'm not sure 'impressed' is the right word," Claudia said, leaning in until her lips mere centimetres from his.

***

Luke smiled and leaned down to kiss her - only to remember at the last millisecond how upset she'd be if he disturbed her vivid crimson lipstick. He tilted his head, and guided his lips down to the side of her throat instead, placing a feather-light kiss on the soft, sensitive skin of her neck.

He felt her shiver in his arms, so he kissed her again and again, to distract her from her nervousness in the most basic way he knew how. His nostrils flared, drawing in a deep lungful of her perfume to sustain him while she was gone. In the last week, he'd discovered a depth of contentment with Claudia that he'd never thought possible. Her scent no longer troubled him like it used to; now, it made him feel relaxed and satisfied.

The intensely lurid visions still bothered him from time to time, but he was no longer upset by them. His reality had become so much more powerful and pleasurable than any fantasy. They were rarely separated for long, and that pleased him because when she was absent he felt as though a piece of his soul was missing. When she returned to him, he felt the simplest kind of joy: the joy of being reunited with his mate.

Although he hadn't said anything to her, Luke was amused by the ironic twist of fate that guided their lives. She had been conceived for the sole purpose of being his mate, and even though they had both rebelled over the idea of their forced union, somehow she ended up being his mate anyway. With her by his side, eternity no longer seemed like a painful burden. Now, it felt like a gift.

But, sometimes he wondered if eternity would be long enough to show her just how much he loved her.

He heard the sound of a heavy door opening, and then she was called by name. Luke slipped his hands up to her shoulders and looked down at her with a smile. "You'll do fine. I love you, and I have faith in you."

"I love you, too," she replied, reaching up to touch his cheek tenderly. "Wait for me?"

His smile deepened. "Always."

Claudia smiled back, then she left him and went to face her destiny alone.

**

The antechamber had been huge and intimidating, but it was nothing compared to the massive meeting room carved into the heart of the mountain. Claudia struggled not to stare but was mostly unsuccessful.

Even after a week, she wasn't used to the scale of everything in the alpine fortress. The room was shaped like a huge cone, its walls painted with astoundingly beautiful Renaissance-style frescoes all the way up to the apex. At that apex was a small stained glass window, which caught the light of the midday sun and cast a colourful reflection on the ground at her feet.

It was high noon, so the effect was particularly breath-taking. Claudia glanced down and studied the pattern on the floor. Suddenly, she realised what it was: it was the *immortelle*, the tiny daisy after which her immortal brethren had named themselves, created by the reflection of sunlight through coloured glass.

She glanced up again, and looked at the centre of the room, which was dominated by a crescent-shaped table made of rich, dark red wood, inlaid with ornate golden metalwork. Around the table sat nine people: five men and four women. In the very centre sat her father. Two seats to his right was Helena, the lady doctor in the Louboutin pumps. All the rest were strangers.

She'd half-expected them to be wearing dramatic hooded robes, but they were just wearing regular clothes. Most were wearing exquisitely-tailored business suits, but there was some variety amongst them. Like her father, their faces were expressionless masks, yet they all radiated power.

"This is her, then?" one of the men said, in crisp, formal German. "She looks like nothing, Edler Herr. Just another mortal."

"And yet, she is my child," Gunther replied in the

same language. "Helena tested her. She is mine."

"Without a shadow of doubt," Helena agreed, nodding.

"She is the spawn of a betrayal." The first man made no attempt to disguise his contempt, waving a dismissive hand in her direction. "I do not understand why we are even considering this."

To her surprise, Gunther defended her. He turned that cold stare of his on the man, tension faintly visible in the set of his jaw. "She's innocent of that betrayal. It was my indiscretion that allowed the betrayal to take place at all. She can't be blamed for that."

The man bristled visibly, but had to take a moment to gather his wits before he could reply. In that moment, Claudia saw her opportunity and stepped forward. In a voice as clear and crisp as a bell, she spoke up and revealed her own fluency in the German tongue. "If I may address the council?"

The entire council froze, and turned to stare at her. Gunther narrowed his eyes and frowned at her. "You didn't tell me you spoke German."

"You didn't ask," she replied, then she pointed at a pile of documents stacked on the table in front of him. "But you do have my academic transcripts. If you examine them further, you'll find that I am also fluent in Italian, French, and Japanese."

Her father glanced down at the papers then looked back up again, and she could see the tension building along his jaw. Just when he seemed about to take offense at her impudence, she smiled brightly, radiantly, and quoted a short phrase. "'To err is human,' Father. Just as each of you once was – and as I am now."

Her father sat back, his expression returning to its neutral mask, and the other council members regarded her with varying degrees of interest. She continued to speak while she had their attention, pacing around the curve of the table so that she could make eye contact with every one of them in turn.

"Once upon a time, each of you stood here before this council, or some relative equivalent," she said. "Remember that. All of you were human once, as I am, young, fragile, and inexperienced. Think about that, and then look through my transcripts." She extended one finger towards the paperwork that documented her life and academic success. "I am twenty-six years old, and yet look how much I've learned and achieved in that time. Think about how much more I have the *potential* to learn and achieve. Consider what I am capable of, if you are but willing to give me the chance.

"I am no enemy of yours. I did not choose my fate, it was chosen for me long before I was born. But I did choose one thing, and that is to stand before you now and offer you a choice of your own. You can either accept me, and I will turn all of my potential towards the betterment of your people—" She paused and looked at her father. "—*our* people. Or, you can send me away. Then we'll never have the chance to know one another, and never have the chance to see just how fruitful this relationship could be."

Her speech completed, Claudia stood back and looked between them, making eye contact with each of them again. One at a time, she analysed their thoughts from their body language, and found them teetering on the edge of the precipice between decisions.

"Well," Helena said, removing her glasses. She looked at Gunther and raised one sculpted eyebrow. "Call me crazy, but I like her. She's got spunk. I say we take her."

"I agree," a second voice chimed in, which belonged to a small, mousy man on the far end who had thus far been silent. "She's educated and well-spoken – so few young people these days can claim that. I believe she would be an asset to us."

Claudia smiled at them and bowed her head in respect to thank them for their vote. Once the first of them had spoken up in her favour, the rest of them fell like dominoes until only one voice remained silent – her father. She looked at him, silent, waiting. Her words had been spoken, and they'd been powerful enough to sway the opinions of the other elders. Only he remained undecided, but his vote could veto all the others if he wanted it to.

Gunther drew a deep breath and closed his eyes for a moment, then nodded his head once. "It's settled, then. You will be granted the gift. It will take us the night to prepare the draught, so we will perform the ceremony at sunrise. Go now, and rest."

The elders began to rise, but Claudia forestalled them hastily. "Wait! What about Luke?"

The group paused, and looked towards their leader for guidance. He stared at her, his expression unreadable. "What about him?"

"Can he stay here?" she asked softly, her body tense even though she was trying very hard not to show it. "He's saved my life more than once, and he brought us together. He could have abandoned me at any time, but he didn't. He deserves better than to be treated as an enemy."

"Do you vouch for him?" Gunther asked, the faintest trace of curiosity dancing through his eyes.

"Yes," she replied without hesitation. "I have never known a man more loyal or more kind. He wants me to marry him, and I'm going to say yes."

Gunther raised an eyebrow. "'Til death do us part' is a long time when you're immortal."

"I know." She smiled suddenly, so radiantly that it practically lit up the room. "But that's the whole point. I want to spend my eternity with him."

For the first time since she'd met him, a ghost of a smile curled the edge of her father's lips. "Then he shall be an adopted son of our clan, unless he proves himself to be otherwise."

Relief flooded through her with such potency that she almost collapsed. "He won't, I'm sure of it. But... thank you."

Claudia dropped into a curtsey, made ever-so-slightly less graceful than normal by her nerves, and then turned and hurried out of the chamber.

***

As promised, Luke was waiting for her outside, his stomach twisting in anxiety. Suddenly, he heard the sound that he'd been waiting for: the click-clack of stiletto heels running towards him. He turned just in time to catch her when she threw herself into his arms. Before he quite knew what was happening, he found himself being lavished with frantic kisses.

When she released him, Luke gently eased her back and looked down into her lovely turquoise eyes, trying to divine the exact nature of her emotion. Her thoughts and feelings were all over the place, and he couldn't work out whether she was happy, sad, or both.

"Tomorrow morning," she told him, blinking back tears. He heaved a sigh and closed his eyes. In that moment, it felt like a burden the size of the Alps themselves had been lifted from his shoulders.

"One last night as a mortal," he said. He drew a deep breath, then opened his eyes and smiled at her.

"One last night." She flashed him a cheeky smile. Her lipstick was smudged, but he didn't mind – he liked her better when she was a little less than perfect. Suddenly, a wicked glimmer passed through her eyes. "Any ideas for what we should do with my one last night as a mortal?"

"Sleep," he replied, straight-faced. "You'll miss it when you don't do it much anymore. As for the other stuff... well, we've got all of eternity now, don't we?"

"Better buy a copy of the Kama Sutra to keep us going, then," she replied, grinning.

Luke laughed and nodded. "Now, that does sound like fun."

Hand in hand, they left the antechamber to go spend her last mortal day together.

Chapter Fifteen

The fateful day dawned clear, though the sky warned of ill weather to come later in the day. Claudia stared up at the threads of fuchsia and gold painted across the cavernous arc of the mid-winter Swiss sky. They were at the peak of the mountain, up so high that the air was thin and the world felt overwhelmingly enormous; by comparison, she felt tiny and inconsequential.

Luke rose from where he'd knelt in the snow beside her to recite their oaths of loyalty, and went to sit off to one side. The oath was complete now. They were members of the Führung Clan. All that was left was the Elixir itself.

Claudia shivered and hugged herself. They were all dressed in light cotton slips for the ceremony, and she was already turning blue from the cold. The elders were all dressed the same way, but none of them showed any signs of discomfort. A perk of their biology, as Luke would say. She glanced back at him and he gave her a reassuring smile, offering her what comfort he could from a distance. She smiled back, and then turned to look at her father.

"This is where your new life begins," Gunther intoned, his voice soft but clear. "Look around you, my daughter: soon all of this will be yours."

His statement was unnecessary — she'd hardly stopped looking since the moment the group had ascended to the highest peak surrounded their little valley. Below them, the Alps spread out as far to the south and east as her eye could see. To the north, the land gradually sloped downwards, towards the rolling foothills and lush plains of the Swiss plateau. The air was so thin she could hardly breathe, but it felt like she could see forever.

She felt a sense of freedom that she could not adequately put a voice to. In a few minutes, she would cast off the shackles of her own mortality and achieve what so many human beings had longed for over the ages. She would become immortal.

Gunther knelt down in the snow in front of her, and held his hand out to her. She glanced at it, then looked up at him quizzically. A faint smile touched his glacial features, and he turned his hand over to reveal a tiny crystal vial twinkling on his palm in the early morning sun.

"I offer you the gift of eternity, my child," he said, his words both ritualistic and poetic. "With this, your new life will begin. No longer will you feel the misery of disease or be lost to the reaper's touch. No more will you be bound by the limits of flesh and blood. Do you accept this gift?"

"I do," she agreed without hesitation. She picked up the vial from his palm and stared down at it with anticipation; the liquid within was clear, like water, but a touch more viscous. It was so small it seemed like nothing, and yet... that tiny thing held the power of eternal life. When she removed the stopper and held it to her lips, she discovered that it had neither odour nor taste. If not for the cool sensation of it sliding down the back of her tongue, she might have suspected the vial was empty.

Claudia closed her eyes and waited. Warmth spread

through her body, as if she'd taken a swig of whiskey. As the minutes ticked by, the feeling crept throughout her limbs, radiating out from her stomach all the way to the tips of her fingers.

The elders had warned her before the ceremony that the elixir would need some time to fully take effect. There were millions of cells in her body and each one of them had to be inscribed with extensive genetic changes. But, rather than overwriting her DNA like a virus, the elixir would unlock the hidden potential within her own genetic code.

And so she sat in meditative silence atop the highest peak of the Swiss Alps. Eventually, she started to get bored, and her mind wandered. She found herself wondering what Piotr was doing. Over the course of the last week, the three youngest members of the clan had struck up a guarded friendship, but it had been solidified with the revelation that both Claudia and Luke would be welcomed into the Führung at last.

To her surprise, her developing psyche found an answer to her unspoken question. Claudia gasped in surprise as her mind's eye shifted and found the trail Piotr's footsteps had left when they fell upon the earth. Cautious but curious, she followed them to where they stopped at the base of the path leading up the mountain, and some new part of her understood that he was waiting there, for them to finish the ritual. She couldn't see what he was doing or hear his thoughts, but she could feel his feet touching the ground as clearly as a friend's voice carried on the wind.

Fascinated, she decided to try another one, and thought of her mother. It came faster this time, more easily. Her mother's footsteps burned like fire on the red earth of Australia, strange and powerful. Claudia felt the pathways she'd walked so many times, and followed them slowly, carefully towards the most recent end of the trail. The path stopped in the dining room of her old home.

She tried to see her mother's face, but this vision was not one of people and places, but of energy and vibration. What she saw was an intense golden glow, radiating power in a strange, subtle sort of way. Close by, there was a softer blue glow that her instincts told her was a mortal, someone whose potential had not yet been unlocked; her mother had a guest.

The warmth in her gut had become a faint burning sensation, but it wasn't painful, just a tiny bit uncomfortable. As Claudia returned to herself, she worried about it for a moment, but she was distracted by the sudden shock when she realised that the cold no longer bothered her at all. She opened her eyes and looked at her father, who merely smiled and nodded, silently encouraging her to be patient. She glanced back at Luke, and she found him watching her as well, observing with the loving dedication of a mate.

When she looked at him, she could feel his connection with the earth as well. He sat upon a low, rocky outcropping, shivering from the cold. She closed her eyes and reached for him with her mind, feeling the soft, masculine sensuality of his presence. Unlike her mother, his energy was dark and pleasant, like a warm blanket on a cold winter's night. She wanted to curl up in it and sleep forever.

Longing filled her heart, so she reached for him with her own essence. He was closer than the others, practically within arm's reach. As she brushed against the edge of his spirit, she realised with shock that she could sense his feelings just as he could feel hers. Even though their physical bodies were metres apart, their souls embraced briefly, tenderly.

When they drew apart, she finally realised that there was another presence there. No, not there – everywhere. It was enormous, all-encompassing, and yet subtle. It was everywhere and nowhere: in the mountains and the trees, in the sky far above them and the oceans far below. She reached out to it tentatively and felt it envelop her, but she experienced no fear because she realised deep in her heart that this presence was part of her birth right.

It was the Power.

Her breath caught in her throat when she felt it embrace her, for in that moment she was everywhere as well. She could feel the mountains below her, enormous, impassive, and cold. She could feel the heat of the magma flowing miles beneath them, surging and throbbing like the pulse of the world. She could feel the touch of the waves crashing against a distant shore, and the patter of hundreds of millions of feet upon the ground. Humans and animals and plants; in one great moment of clarity, she felt them all.

The Power was the thread that bound them all in an intricate web, too intricate for her demi-mortal mind to comprehend. With great difficulty, she withdrew herself from the mighty essence and focused on her one small corner of the world. The Power followed her like a curious puppy; when she returned to the mountain, it came with her.

It radiated consciousness on a level too vast for her to truly understand. She felt that it was alive, but not really self-aware. It was ancient, though – perhaps as old as the world itself – and it was aware of her without truly being sentient. It curled around her, obediently waiting for her command. She felt like she could bend it to her will, but she didn't know how.

Small and gentle compared to its eternal might, she reached out to the Power and touched it, caressing it with the softest edge of her own essence.

"I do not know how to do this," she admitted silently, projecting the words with her mind. She felt a subtle sense of understanding, and then suddenly she was being guided, like a loving parent guides a child. Together, they touched the cold ground and willed it to become warm, so that her beloved would not have to shiver any longer. Feelings of love and affection sprang up from deep within her soul and radiated out through the Power all around her. As though delighted by those feelings, the Power responded to her call.

Her eyes still closed, the first warning she got that anything was amiss was the gasps of surprise from the people all around her. When she opened her eyes, she found herself blinded by mist. The ground beneath her had become warm, pleasantly warm, and the snow had melted away with preternatural swiftness.

She stared around in wonder: as the mist rolled away and oozed down the mountainside, it left nothing behind it but stone and bare earth – the deep, mid-winter snows were gone. Stunned by her own power, Claudia glanced at the elders for a moment, and saw that they bore expressions that ranged from concern through to pleasure.

Then she felt the Power waiting for her, to show her what else she could do. Her fright was forgotten in a moment of childlike glee. She threw back her head and laughed, reaching out to the Power again. This time, she embraced it wholeheartedly and thrust her essence deep within its boundless presence. The Power wrapped itself around her and welcomed her in, and they dove deep into the spirit of the earth.

Together, they found the tiny seeds discarded by flowers the previous summer, and filled them with their Power. Plants leapt forth from the earth in a rippling, trembling green wave, covering the mountainside and deep down into the vale. A moment later, they burst into bloom, unfurling a rainbow of brightly-coloured petals.

Claudia gasped for breath as she emerged from the Power and returned to her body, only to find herself dripping wet. While she'd been focused on the flowers, the mist had become clouds, and the clouds became rain, a veritable spring shower in the middle of winter.

She tilted her head back and stared up at the rain clouds, as though seeing them for the very first time. In some ways, she was. Never before had she seen the pulse of the Power wending through the atmosphere. Wide-eyed, like a child reborn, she stared and stared, taking in every aspect of the new world revealed to her. Although she could hear people speaking around her, she wasn't paying attention to them.

As suddenly as the Power had come to her, it slipped away again and left her feeling momentarily bereaved. The feeling passed swiftly though, when she realised that it wasn't gone completely, but had retreated back to where it belonged. It felt like she had made a new friend, and that friend had gone into another room for a while, to leave her alone with her own thoughts.

No, she wasn't alone. Luke was there. Her Luke, sweet and caring. She could feel his presence, the tender touch of his essence close against her own. When she shifted her focus back to the people around her, he was sitting beside her, holding her so that she wouldn't slip to the ground. Still stunned by her experience, she stared at him without really seeing his face. She didn't need to. She could feel him in a way that was much more profound than ever before.

The need to rest began to overwhelm her, but she fought against it with every aspect of her being. She wanted to stay awake, to tell her love everything that she'd seen and felt. She wanted to share the experience with him, but she couldn't. The longer she tried to keep her eyes open, the more difficult it became.

Eventually, the part of her that was still conscious realised that her body needed rest, and so she succumbed to blessed sleep.

***

Luke caught Claudia when she fainted, and gathered her up close against his chest. He shot a worried glance towards her father, but the elder showed no concern.

"Don't worry, that usually happens," Gunther said, leaning back to regard the havoc Claudia had caused. "This is new, though."

"It certainly will be interesting to explain to the villagers," Helena commented dryly. Luke glanced at her and found her smiling, a twinkle of pleasure in her eyes that he hadn't seen since they'd met. As he looked around at the others, he saw she was not the only one. Even Gunther's stony expression had been replaced by a smile. The elders looked invigorated and revitalised, as if their bond with the Power had been renewed.

"Piotr's going to be jealous," Gunther said. "When he first joined us, he almost created a volcano on this very spot. It took all of our combined efforts to stop him."

Luke glanced around, at the flowers that spread across the entire mountain range and down deep into the valley and plains beyond. It was a riot of colours, beautiful and alive in a way that he'd never seen before – much like Claudia herself. The flower heads bobbed and swayed in the breeze, splattered by fat raindrops.

Then there was Claudia. She lay in his arms, her eyelids twitching faintly, clad only in a white slip that was left faintly translucent by the rain. He felt the stirring of desire in his belly, but it was overcome by a protective need. As gently as he could, he drew her into his lap and held her against him, to preserve her modesty in some small way.

Luke felt peculiar. As the youngest of his clan, he'd never witnessed an initiation besides his own, which was a memory he looked at with disdain. Claudia's had felt so different. When she'd called on the Power, he had sensed it too – not just through their bond, but in the world all around her. He'd never felt the Power with such clarity before.

He had watched in mute shock when she summoned it for the first time, for in all his life he'd never seen anything so incredible, or so beautiful. The Power had come to her with a grace and a trust that he'd never imagined was possible, and they had worked together as one to paint a picture of astounding beauty. Now that it was over, he felt a strange combination of buoyancy and dismay. He felt uplifted, but also in awe and a little bit troubled. He feared that immortality would change her, and make her less than the woman he knew.

"So," Gunther said suddenly, interrupting his thoughts. Luke glanced up, and realised that the elder was watching him intently. "You're going to marry my daughter?"

Luke summoned an awkward, lopsided smile, and shrugged. "I already bought her a ring, but she said it was too early to ask. So, it's up to her, really."

"She'll understand soon enough that time has no meaning to our kind," Gunther replied, rising to his feet with a grace that belied his true age. "In the meantime, we must organise her training regime. It seems that she wields a great deal of power; we must rein it in lest it become destructive."

"I don't think you have to worry about that," Luke said with a smile. "We've shared a bond for some time now. There isn't a destructive bone in her body."

"Regardless, she must be trained," Gunther said with a shrug. "It is our way. Until she awakes, I leave her in your care. Helena will be available if you require her services."

Luke nodded silently and stared down at the face that he held so dear while the elders filed away, then he gathered her up and carried her back down the mountain, to rest and recover in their new castle home.

Epilogue

The box hit the ground with a terrible crash, right on top of Luke's foot. He yelped in pain and danced away, while Claudia laughed merrily at his misfortune.

"I told you that was too big to carry all by yourself," she mocked, wagging a finger at him. "Just wait for Piotr; he'll be here any minute."

"Some girlfriend you are. I have a war-wound! Where's my sympathy?" Luke complained, but the pain was fading fast and with it his good mood returned. In the four months that had passed since Claudia had become immortal, he'd never been happier.

His initial concerns had proven to be completely unfounded. She'd taken to immortality like a duck to water, and shown no sign of losing that precious bloom of life which had attracted him in the first place. He could only pray it would stay that way forever, and that she would not become jaded and hard as the years progressed. Either way, it didn't seem to matter in the here and now. Like the tiny, everlasting *immortelle*, their love had blossomed in their time in Switzerland. Although she still spent much of her time ensconced in training with her elders, they always found time to spend together one way or another.

They often laughed and joked about what she'd done in her first moments of immortality; rumours still abounded amongst the mortals about why spring had come to Europe so early and so suddenly that year. It was the first time in living memory that the tulips in the Netherlands had burst into bloom in mid-February.

While Claudia was trapped in study, Luke spent his days out amongst nature, exploring all the beauty it had to offer. He found himself so inspired that he'd begun work on his very first manuscript. Although he considered it a poor effort at best, Claudia praised him endlessly for trying, and her praise kept him going.

Eventually, Claudia's control of the Power finally reached a point that the elders agreed that it was safe for them to move out of the castle if they chose to. Luke had suggested they buy a house together, and Claudia had found the idea enchanting. It had taken a while to choose the perfect house, but when they finally found the tiny cottage nestled in the crook of the hills overlooking the Swiss plateau, they both knew they'd finally come home.

"No sympathy for you," Claudia taunted. "'Use the servants, Claudia,' you say, 'We pay them for a reason. Let them do their jobs.' Lecture, lecture, lecture – and the one day we actually need their help, who's the one too stubborn to hire movers?"

"And now she's mocking the wounded?" Luke cried in mock-horror. "Unbelievable!"

He feigned a gasp and leapt at her, but she darted away before he could catch her. He gave chase and she fled from him, squealing with gleeful abandon. Then she took a wrong turn into a hallway packed full of boxes, and she was caught. With no regard for propriety, he swept her off her feet and twirled her around, then pinned her up against a wall and kissed her hard.

She returned the kiss with equal enthusiasm, and twisted her fingers in the thin fabric of his shirt. Their lips parted and left them flushed and breathless, gazing at one another with longing.

"How long until Piotr gets here, again?" Claudia whispered, slipping one hand beneath his shirt to trail her fingertips across his stomach.

Luke shivered and heaved a sigh. "Not nearly long enough, I'm afraid."

"Pity." She sighed as well and extracted her hand reluctantly. Ever since she'd joined the ranks of the immortals, Claudia's stamina had grown to almost match Luke's. There was no such thing as a quickie anymore, not when their lovemaking could last all day if they wanted it to.

"How about we do something else, instead?" he suggested with a grin, sliding his arm around her waist to keep her close.

"What kind of something?" she asked, tilting her head up to look him in the eye. There was no keeping secrets from her now, their bond was much too strong. She knew the moment he tried to hide his thoughts from her. Still, he only needed a few seconds to surprise her, and that was enough.

"Well..." he said, drawing out the suspense for as long as he could. "We could play chess... build a couch fort, or maybe..." A tiny black box appeared as if by magic from his pocket. "...we could get engaged?"

He popped it open to reveal the engagement ring inside, a slender, tasteful platinum band with a single, beautiful diamond. He'd chosen it with great care to appeal to her conscientious nature. It was neither showy nor tacky, but it was exquisitely well-crafted.

Claudia's smile lit up the room. "It's about time. I was starting to think you'd forgotten."

"Is that a yes, then?" Luke asked. "Or are you going to make me get down on one knee?"

"Would I do that to you? Of course it's a yes." She smiled at him, then lunged for the box. "Now, gimme!"

"Ah-ah-ah." Luke held it up high, just beyond her reach. "You have to earn it first. Where's my kiss?"

"Hey, no kiss, no kiss," Piotr protested from the doorway, startling them both. When they turned towards him, he spotted the little ring box that was their bone of contention, and a broad smile spread across his face. "Ah, finally. You give to her?"

"Well, I was going to, but—" Luke started to say as a joke, only to yelp in protest when Claudia took advantage of his momentary distraction to grab the box. "—hey!"

"Mine!" Claudia told him smugly and danced away to the kitchen, leaving the men staring after her in amusement. A moment later, she returned – carrying *two* ring boxes. "Actually, I got you one as well. I know it's not very traditional, but I remember reading stories from the war, about men who used to carry their engagement rings into battle so they could keep their sweethearts close to them while they were away. I thought it might strike a chord with you."

Luke was both surprised and pleased by the gift. The ring she gave him was a simple band, delicate and tasteful, the ideal match for hers. He stared at it for a long moment, then looked up at her and smiled. "It does. Thank you, my love."

"Excellent, is settled now." Piotr clapped them both on the shoulders simultaneously, grinning. "I will be your maid of honour, yes? Good. Now, come, much unpacking to do."

The enormous Polish man trundled off out the door, leaving Claudia and Luke staring after him in bewilderment. Suddenly, the humour of his words struck them and they both melted down into laughter.

With so much to do and all of eternity to do it in, they put their rings in a safe place, side by side, and rushed off to help Piotr bring in the furnishings of their new life together.

***

A few kilometres away, in his office overlooking the valley, Gunther indulged himself in a long, deep sigh. It seemed like all the indiscretions of his past were coming back to haunt him, though at least the one which had resulted in Claudia's birth had turned out for the best. This new one, though… it was going to be trouble. He just knew it.

A knock on the door interrupted his thoughts. He glanced up, and called out permission to enter. "Come in, Helena."

The door opened and Helena hurried inside, wearing a frown almost as deep as his own. "Edler Herr, we have a problem."

"Unless you're talking about the problem I'm already dealing with, that means we have *two* problems," he replied, struggling to hide his annoyance. He waved a hand towards one of the chairs on the far side of his desk. "I've just received some troubling information regarding Viktor Grekov."

"Viktor Grekov? The Slavic elder?" Helena asked, raising one eyebrow. "He's the one that you have… history with, isn't he?"

"History?" Gunther grimaced and shook his head. "I suppose that's one way to describe it, yes. I've just received evidence that he was involved in a troubling incident during World War II, which would put him in direct violation of the Immortelle Accord."

"Oh dear," Helena said, glancing down at her hands.

"What kind of incident are we talking about? The kind that we have to respond to?"

"Unfortunately, yes," Gunther replied. "The evidence suggests he was directly responsible for the massacre of more than twenty thousand Polish nationals. The evidence is very convincing. We have to address the charges, or our Polish members will be furious... which means that we're going to have to bring Viktor here for a trial."

"The Slavs aren't going to like that," Helena said quietly, her expression understandably tense. "They're already furious at us because of the trade sanctions. This could ignite a war."

"And if I don't, the council may hold me responsible for failing to address the charges," he replied, rubbing his forehead with his fingers. "I need time to think about the best way to handle this before it gets out to the rest of the Clan. What's the problem that you mentioned?"

"Well, it's not as worrisome as a potential war with the Slavs, if that makes you feel any better," she said dryly. "I was just doing an inventory of our laboratories, and discovered several of the blood samples we had on ice are missing. One of them is Claudia's."

Gunther bit his tongue to keep from swearing out loud, his hands tightening into fists. "When?"

"We don't know," she admitted. "One of our cryogenic transport units is missing, too, so it's a safe bet that the thief knew how to keep the genetic material viable. Let's just hope that the Cabal were responsible, not the Slavs. I don't need to tell you what that would mean."

"I know," Gunter replied. "A potential army of doppelgangers. Not what we need if we have to go to war. See what you can find out, and keep me appraised."

Helena rose from her seat, bowed, and departed in a hurry, leaving him alone with a headache and a troubling dilemma. Which was worse? Going to war against an old friend, or knowing that someone out there had the potential to cause great harm to his only daughter and he was powerless to stop it?

The World of the Immortelle

Earth seems like such a simple place in the modern age. Science has explained away the mysteries of the universe. There are no surprises. Most people laugh off the idea of secret societies and conspiracy theories as the work of fools and madmen.

The problem is, the madmen are right.

The world is secretly ruled a select group of violent and ruthless immortals that call themselves the Immortelle. These men and women were mortal once, until a mysterious elixir unlocked the greatest potential hidden within their own genetic codes. The exact nature of that power is determined by their own biological origins, but they are ancient, powerful and bow to no mortal.

Absolute power corrupts absolutely, but in the world of the Immortelle nothing is ever as black or white as it seems.

At First Blush

Dawn Fitzpatrick #1

***

Normality was never going to be a big part of Dawn's life. She was only five years old when she discovered that the world was not as it seems. One day, she's playing on the beach when she meets a mysterious young boy named Cijal. There's just one thing that separates him from all her other, normal friends: Cijal is not human.

Although they don't even speak the same language, Dawn is fascinated by the strange boy that lives beneath the sea. They find friendship together, and spend their summers playing in the sand, forming the kind of bond that no amount of dissimilarities can possibly break.

Then, at the age of twelve, a terrible tragedy separates Dawn from her childhood sweetheart without giving her the chance to say goodbye. How can she move on without closure? How can she forget him? As she grows, her memories become fractured and distant, and she even begins to wonder if she just imagined him.

Finally, her eighteenth birthday comes and she is free of the shackles of childhood – free to choose her own path. She goes in search of him, hoping to recapture the one last happy memory of her childhood. But Cijal is from a completely different world. He's a Nereidis, a member of a powerful, super-human race of amphibians who live secretly beneath the waves.

In her heart, she needs to see him again – to know that he's real, and not just a dream. But how can an ordinary human being hope to find an amphibian that has the entire ocean to hide in?

And if she does find him, how could they possibly construct a life together?

Love Thy Enemy

Anya Karekanova #1

***

Anya was destined for a life of poverty and misery, until a chance meeting swept her up into the mysterious world of the undying Immortelle. Now, forty years later, she has become one of them: the student, lover, and protégée of the elder, Viktor Grekov.

She calls him 'master' and he calls her 'pet', but there is nothing subservient about their relationship. Anya is no one's pet. She is a member of the dark and violent Slavic Clan that secretly dominate Russia and the territories of the former Soviet Union from behind the veil of secrecy that surrounds all of the Immortelle. Because of her Siberian blood, she possesses the bloody ability to perform fleshcraft. She can manipulate of flesh of living things to suit her whim. But, that is only part of who Anya is.

Anya Karekanova is a half-breed.

While her mother's Siberian blood links her to the Slavic Clan's abilities, her father's ties her to the sensual and charismatic Cabalist bloodlines. The Cabal, who use the Power to manipulate the minds of their victims, and thrive on sex. Half shape-shifter and half empath, Anya must learn to balance the two warring halves of her nature in order to best serve her chosen allies.

In the midst of her internal turmoil, two new men enter her life to complicate things. Twin brothers, the sons of her clan's oldest enemies, invited to Moscow to engage in peace talks that could finally build a lasting peace between their clans. Except talking isn't the only thing the twins are interested in.

Then, just when things seem to be going well, an unexpected betrayal turns everything on its head, and Anya must fight to defend her oldest enemies – and herself – from a deadly threat.

About The Author

Born in Auckland, New Zealand, Victoria Dreyer began her career in the most peculiar of ways - as the writer and illustrator of graphic novels. Although her ultimate dream was always to become a novelist, she spent many years exploring other mediums before finally returning to the one she felt most comfortable with - the written word.

Ms Dreyer is a voracious reader, and in addition to the post-apocalyptic genre she also enjoys reading and writing science fiction, modern fantasy, and the paranormal romance genres. Her primary works include the *Survivors* series under the moniker V. L. Dreyer, the *Immortelle* series under the moniker Abigail Hawk, and numerous short stories.

She currently resides in West Auckland with several flatmates, a large collection of books and two very spoilt cats.

www.ingramcontent.com/pod-product-compliance
Lightning Source LLC
Chambersburg PA
CBHW020422180626
46812CB00003B/1110